# TAKE OFF YOUR COAT AND SLAY AWHILE . . .

"I think the cabin's deserted," Frank said. "It's as good a place as any to stop and rest."

Fear welled up in Holly's eyes. "Those men," she said, her lips trembling. "They'll find us. They'll catch us."

"No, Frank's right," replied Joe. "We don't even know for sure if we're being followed. It's what's ahead that we have to be prepared for. Go on in, you'll be safe."

Holly nodded, then vanished into the cabin.

Frank sighed. "Looks like we're on our own."

A scream ripped from the cabin.

"Holly!" Frank cried. Unsheathing his knife, he kicked in the cabin door. Holly was on the floor, crawling backward toward him. Her shrieks filled the air, but he couldn't see what she was shrieking at.

Then a creature with matted hair and mad eyes rose from the floor. . . .

# THE HARDY BOYS CASEFILES™ NO. 3

# CULT OF CRIME

### FRANKLIN W. DIXON

## GREY CASTLE PRESS

Library edition:
## GARETH STEVENS PUBLISHING

First Grey Castle Edition, Lakeville, Connecticut, September, 1988

Published in Large Print by arrangement with Simon & Schuster, Inc.

Printed in the U.S.A.

**Library of Congress Cataloging-in-Publication Data**

Dixon, Franklin W.
Cult of crime.

(The Hardy Boys casefiles ; no. 3)
Summary: In trying to free their friend Holly from the clutches of a murderous mountain cult, the Hardy Boys find that the lunatic Rajah and his followers have spread to their own home town.
1. Large type books. [1. Cults—Fiction. 2. Mystery and detective stories. 3. Large type books] I. Title. II. Series: Dixon, Franklin W. Hardy Boys casefiles ; no. 3.
[PZ7.D644Cu 1988]    [Fic]    88-21366
ISBN 0-942545-44-3 (lg. print)
ISBN 0-942545-54-0 (lib. bdg.: lg. print) .

# CULT OF CRIME

# Chapter
## 1

HE WANDERED AIMLESSLY as night fell on the New York City streets. The growling in his stomach reminded him of how long it had been since he'd eaten last. Though tall, he stooped when he walked, and even when trying to beg money from passersby, he could no longer look other people in the eye.

Like many other teenagers who had left home and come to the city, he owned nothing but the clothes on his back. And he was homeless, with nowhere to go.

He searched for a place to spend the night. He had no money to spend on a hotel, and he had learned long ago that if he went to a shelter, the authorities would learn his age and his name and send him home.

He hoped he could find a doorway or an alley-

1

way with a cardboard box to sleep in, but he was wary of the other people who slept on the streets. They didn't like strangers, and choosing a spot that one of them had already chosen could get him beaten, or even killed. He kept walking.

The bells were what startled him. It seemed strange to him that something so beautiful could be heard in a neighborhood of rundown buildings and vacant lots, where honest people didn't come out at night, and where thieves and rats and insects crawled the streets.

But there they were. Rhythmically they grew louder, then softer, then louder again, like some low, lovely song, and he found himself drawn to them.

He was almost at the building before he realized it. The building rose out of the slums like a beacon, and men and women—boys and girls, really, as none of them were older than he was—chanted and swayed both inside it and on the street in front of it.

The men wore white tunics tied at the waist with a sash and long, white slacks that reached down to the cloth sandals on their feet. The women had scarves wrapped around their heads and wore long, white gowns covering them from shoulder to ankle.

They were happy, all of them. He could see it in their faces. They danced in the glow of the neon lights on the front of the building, the lights that read Mission.

2

It was a church, unlike any he had ever seen in the little town of Bayport.

He wanted to back away, to run, but the smell of food wafted out of the building. He inhaled hungrily, and on his stomach's command, his feet marched forward. He moved out of the shadows and into the light.

The dancing stopped and the bells died. Everyone was looking at him.

He felt awkward. These people in their pure white clothes were everything he was not. He ran a filthy hand through his brown hair, and grime fell from it. Again he wanted to run, but the stares and the scent of food sapped him of strength, and without even thinking, he reached out his hands.

"Please," he croaked, and he could feel the tears welling up in his eyes. What right did he have to expect their help or to share their food?

He didn't even have to look in their eyes to know what would be there: the same disgust and fear he had seen in the eyes of everyone he had ever asked for help since he came to the city. He hated that look.

A young woman touched him gently on the shoulder.

She was smiling serenely, and on her face he saw none of the fear he had expected. Instead there was kindness. It was in her eyes and in her touch, and for the first time since leaving home, he felt warm inside. He felt almost as if he had come home again.

"You're tired," she said, and he nodded mutely. Her eyes were a deep blue, and her skin was smooth and white. There was peace in the graceful way she moved, and her outstretched hand seemed to offer him that peace. "You can sleep in the mission tonight. And have plenty of food. Would you like some supper?"

Before he could answer, the others surrounded him. They laughed and smiled and slapped him gently on the back, as if he were an old friend. He nodded fiercely and smiled back, and before he knew it, they were all going into the building.

"What's your name?" he asked the woman. His throat hurt, and he realized that he had barely spoken since arriving in the city.

"Chandra," she replied.

"Chandra," he repeated. "I thought you were American, but that name sounds—"

"Indian," she cut in. "I used to have another name, but that was before I received the Rajah's peace."

Inside, the building was almost empty. He could smell food coming from somewhere—a kitchen, probably—but in the main room he saw nothing but rows and rows of woven flaxen mats, with a wooden bowl set in front of each. One by one, and one on each mat, the boys and girls sat down, crossing their legs underneath them.

Chandra led him to an empty mat and then sat on the mat next to it.

"The Rajah's peace?" he said, looking at her

4

with suspicion. "This isn't one of those crazy cults, is it? I don't want to get hooked up with that kind of thing."

Chandra smiled at him again, and the smile washed away his fears. "Don't worry, brother. We make no one stay against his will. When you are fed and rested, you can return to the world if you like. But I pray that the Rajah's peace will bless you, too."

A large lump of rice dropped into his bowl, dumped there by a boy who carried a large pot and a ladle. He reached down to scoop it into his mouth, but Chandra put a hand on his wrist and kept him from raising it again.

"Not yet," she said. "We have to wait, but not long. Do you like the city?"

He sunk his head to his chest and took a deep breath. He could feel tears welling up in his eyes. "I hate it," he said.

"But you can't go home," she replied. It was a statement, not a question. "I came to the city like you once, and I ended up like you. One thing saved me."

"What's that?"

"The Rajah." Her eyes seemed to glow as she spoke the name. "He has a place far from here, out in the country. It's a place where we return to the natural way, where we can be cleansed of the evil of the city and of this society."

Chandra stared straight into his eyes, and her fingers brushed his cheek. For a moment he felt

5

as if his heart would stop. "You can go there, if you like," she continued. "Our bus leaves in the morning."

"I don't know," he replied. There was suspicion in his voice, but she didn't seem to mind.

"Be calm," she said. "We're happy, and we only want you to be happy. You want to be happy, don't you?"

"Well . . ." He sighed and thought of his days on the street. He remembered the cold and the hunger and the scornful looks. Finally he admitted, "Yes."

"The Rajah can make you happy," Chandra said. "You don't have to stay. You can leave any time you want. But if you really want to be happy, all you have to do is get on that bus."

"Well, well. What have we here?" a deep voice boomed above him. He looked up to see a golden-haired man wrapped in gold-and-scarlet robes. The man gazed down at him with fire in his eyes.

"Who's he?" he murmured to Chandra. She bowed where she sat, her face to the floor and her arms outstretched before her.

"Vivasvat, the right hand of the Rajah," she whispered. "All glory to Vivasvat."

A strong hand gripped his collar and lifted him up, and he found himself gawking at the man in scarlet and gold. "This filthy boy has no place in the Rajah's temple!" Vivasvat shouted. The room grew silent. "He is unclean."

Then Vivasvat shook him, and dirt flaked off

him and fell on the floor. The others began to laugh, and Vivasvat grinned and let him go.

"Unclean things cannot stand the light of the Rajah's truth. Take him upstairs and bathe him," Vivasvat ordered two boys who sat nearby. "Burn his clothes and give him our finest garments to wear. For only when he is purified are we pure, and only then shall we eat the Rajah's food."

The boys each took him by an arm and began to hustle him out of the room. They had almost reached a door leading to stairs when Vivasvat's voice boomed again.

"Boy!" he said. "What is your name?"

"Frank," he replied. "Frank Hardy."

Then they whisked him through the door and up the steps.

# Chapter

## 2

WHEN THE BUS pulled away from the building the next morning, Frank Hardy was on it. He was dressed as all the others were dressed, and anyone would have mistaken him for one of the Rajah's followers, except that his hair was thick and full while theirs had been cut short.

Long ago, the bus had been a school bus, but the Rajah's followers had transformed it. They'd painted it, and slogans praising the Rajah were written all over the walls. Smiling, happy faces beamed all around him.

This is where I have to be careful, Frank thought. A dinner and a breakfast that were heavy on starch, new clothes, getting up early in the morning. They never let me out of their sight, and they try to keep me involved in their activities. They want to break down my defenses. I can't let them. For Holly's sake, *I can't let them.*

"Let's pass the time with a sing-along," a jolly voice said. Cheers greeted the suggestion. Slowly someone started singing a familiar melody, and the song sped up as more people joined in.

Chandra, seated in front of him, turned around. "Join in, Frank," she said. "It's fun."

He smiled and nodded. Blot it out, he told himself. Don't play their mind games. Think about something else. Try to remember what you're trying to do, how you got here.

"Join in, Frank," Chandra repeated, and immediately other voices chimed in, crying, "Join in, Frank. Join in."

In his mind, he drifted away, while his lips began to mouth the words of the song. And without realizing it, he began to smile. In his mind, Frank Hardy could see his family's house in Bayport. It was an old house, built around the turn of the century, but it was large and warm in a way that more modern buildings never were. It was home. He and his brother, Joe, had grown up there, as had their father, the famous detective Fenton Hardy, and his father before him.

Was it only a week since Frank had been home? It seemed as if years had passed since the morning Emmett Strand had come to their door.

The weather had been unseasonably hot, and Frank, a light sleeper at the best of times, tossed and turned in his bed all night. He had dozed on and off for hours, getting up now and then to play a game of chess with his computer in the hopes that it would tire him out.

Someone was moving about downstairs. Frank knew it wasn't a burglar, because the alarms hadn't gone off. He had put in the security system himself, so he knew the alarms worked. More likely, the "prowler" was either Joe or his father, who had been out of town on a case.

Frank felt like going downstairs for a chat, but that wouldn't help him sleep. He pressed his face into his pillow and closed his eyes.

He was finally drifting off when a loud pounding on the front door of the house jarred him awake again. He looked at the digital clock on his nightstand. 5:03 A.M. No one comes around at this time of morning, he thought. He leaped out of bed and threw on his robe. Not unless there's trouble.

Frank heard the front door creak open. Footsteps echoed on the wooden floor of the foyer by the door. He opened the door to his room and jumped back.

Joe was on the other side of the door. He was an inch shorter than Frank, and his blond hair was matted down on his head. Though a year younger than his brother, Joe was the huskier of the two. In the dim light of the hall, his blue eyes gleamed with surprise. They had both startled each other.

"What are you doing out here, Joe?" Frank

whispered. He sighed with relief. "Why aren't you asleep?"

"I *can't* sleep," Joe replied. "It's too hot, and I had this funny feeling that something was going to happen. It looks like I was right. Dad got home half an hour ago and called Mr. Strand. He just came over."

"Emmett Strand? The banker?"

"Right," Joe said through a yawn. "And since I couldn't sleep, I sneaked downstairs to find out what Dad was up to these days. I think he's been doing some work for Mr. Strand, but it sounded like Dad couldn't finish the case."

Frank blinked with surprise. "That's not like Dad. Let's try to find out what's going on." Quietly they slipped down the hall, passing their mother's room and then their Aunt Gertrude's. Both women were sleeping soundly. The boys crept down the stairway to the main floor, trying hard to keep the old steps from creaking.

From the stairs they could see that a desk lamp was on in their father's office. Mr. Strand was there, too, pacing back and forth and dabbing the sweat from his face with a handkerchief. His eyes were wide and dulled with worry, and frustration and fear could be heard in his voice.

In all the years Frank had known Emmett Strand, he had never seen him display the slightest uneasiness. Mr. Strand ran his life as he ran his business—with clear logic and very little emotion—and that style had made him one of the top bankers on the East Coast. Not even when his wife died, leaving him to raise their infant daughter alone, did Strand let his emotions run away with him.

"Maybe I should have been more like you," Strand was saying as the Hardys moved closer to the door. His voice cracked as he spoke. "Your boys turned out all right. Isn't there *anything* we can do?"

"I'm afraid not, Emmett," Fenton Hardy replied. "And there's nothing the police can do, either. Holly's of age now, which means you can't control her anymore. We can always hope she'll change her mind, but in the meantime, you'd better protect yourself."

*Holly?* Frank was surprised. She was Strand's daughter, and she and Frank had grown up together. Before he'd met Callie Shaw, he had even thought that they might fall in love one day. Apparently she was now in some kind of trouble—trouble so bad that even his father couldn't get her out of it.

"What do you mean, protect myself?" Emmett Strand asked.

"I wish I didn't have to bring this up," Mr. Hardy said. "But keep in mind that Holly hasn't simply run away from home. She has joined a cult. This man who runs it, the Rajah, demands that his followers turn over all their worldly goods to him. That's the first step on their path to 'enlightenment.' "

"Hah!" Strand snorted. "If he hates worldly goods so much, why does he have a fleet of Cadillacs? He's a con man, pure and simple."

"Maybe so, but that's not the point."

"What *is* the point, Fenton?"

"The point is, Emmett," Mr. Hardy replied, "that you've made millions in banking. Suppose something should happen to you. Who'd inherit the money and everything else you own?"

There was a long pause as Strand sank into a chair. Finally he replied, "Holly, of course."

"And in her present frame of mind, I think she'd turn it all over to the Rajah," Fenton Hardy went on. "Everything you worked for all these years would be in the Rajah's hands. You've got to cut Holly out of your will, at least until she comes home."

"I can't!" Strand exclaimed in anguish. "She's my only child. I can't cut her off just like that, even though she has cut me out of her life. There must be something else we can do."

"Face facts," said Fenton Hardy gently. "Holly is living at the Rajah's commune upstate. If there was a chance that you could convince her to come home, I wouldn't have to suggest this. But I know they won't even let you in to talk to her. I traced her up there, but I can't go in and get her without breaking the law, and neither can the police."

"The law! The law protects that . . . that thief! Doesn't the law care about my daughter?"

13

Hardy patted his friend's shoulder, trying to comfort him. "I know this is hard for you, Emmett—"

Emmett Strand stood up abruptly, shaking off the hand. "I've been a bad father, but I won't abandon my daughter when she needs me most. I won't do what you're suggesting!"

"Emmett, please!"

"I won't, Fenton! And it doesn't matter if you refuse to rescue Holly. I'll find someone who will. I'll do it myself if I have to!" With that, Emmett Strand turned on his heel and stormed out of Fenton Hardy's office, and out of the house.

On the stairs, Frank whispered, "Let's get back to our rooms before Dad finds out we've been eavesdropping."

But Joe stood where he was, clenching his fists, his lips curled in anger. "That Rajah character is stealing Holly's life just like the Assassins stole Iola's. Maybe he's not killing her like Iola was killed, but she's lost to us just the same. I wish there was something we could do to help her."

Frank Hardy rubbed his chin, thinking over what he had heard. "Maybe there is," he said. "Maybe there is."

"Are you sure you want to go through with this?" Joe asked Frank as the train carried them toward New York City. "This cult stuff gets pretty strange. Suppose you knuckle under to them, the way Holly did.''

''It won't happen,'' Frank replied. He wore old, crumpled clothes, and dirt smudged his face. ''I've studied how cults work and how they brainwash the kids who fall into their hands. But those kids desperately want the approval the cult gives them. I don't. As long as I keep my mind on what I'm there for, they won't have any power over me.''

Joe frowned. ''I still don't like it. We should just bust in there and get her out.''

''We can't. It's illegal,'' Frank said. ''Besides, when I get in there to talk to her, I'm sure I can convince her to leave with me. If she leaves of her own free will, then we won't be breaking the law.''

''*If* you get in. They're going to be suspicious if you just walk up and ask to go to their commune.''

Frank smiled mischievously. ''I don't need to ask them. They'll ask me. I know how their minds work. Once I'm in, they'll want to get me somewhere where the only influence on me is the Rajah, where they can watch my every move and make sure I'm trying to be like them. And the only place for that is the commune.''

''I still don't like it,'' Joe said, scowling. ''What if something goes wrong?''

''That's why you're backing me up, little

15

brother." What could go wrong? Frank thought. I'm wise to their tricks, and if I don't fall for them, they'll have no power over me.

It had seemed like such sound reasoning at the time. . . .

"Frank!" Chandra said, shaking him. His eyes snapped open, and he was aware that the singing had stopped. Every eye in the bus was on him, demanding his attention.

"You mustn't sleep, Frank," she continued. Her smile turned gentle again. "It isn't time for that. To be enlightened, we must become truly awake, and to do that we must fight sleep, which is the enemy of wisdom."

"I'm sorry," he said, and to his astonishment, he *was* sorry. He didn't know the people he was with, but what they thought of him was becoming important to him. He studied their faces. There was a joy and serenity in them that he had not expected.

They couldn't all be faking it, he thought. Maybe they do know something we don't. Maybe they have connected with a new spirituality.

He shook himself suddenly. I'm falling for it. I knew exactly what to expect and I'm still falling for it. A quiet fear began to gnaw at him. He tried to remember things like Bayport and Joe, but already those things seemed somewhat remote.

"Are you all right, Frank?" Chandra said with concern.

"I'm just feeling a little sick," he replied. Before he could say anything more, she was calling for the driver to stop the bus. It skidded to a halt on the gravel siding of the road, and Frank was hustled off, surrounded by cultists who blocked every avenue of escape.

"Get some air," Chandra ordered. "When you're feeling well enough, we'll continue." If the truth were known, Frank felt better already.

For he had seen, a quarter of a mile or so down the road in back of them, a black van. It was the van that the Bayport Mall Merchants had presented to the Hardys after the *Dead on Target* case, when Frank and Joe had thwarted a terrorist bombing and assassination attempt in the heart of the mall. Now, to Frank, it was proof that Joe was really there after all, watching out for him.

As Frank watched, a small car pulled in front of the black van and stopped dead, forcing the van to stop as well. Two men hopped out of the car. They were dressed in the white tunics and slacks that the Rajah's followers wore. But the sunlight glinted off the guns in their hands.

# Chapter

## 3

JOE HARDY DROVE the black van down winding mountain roads. Ever since the Rajah's bus had left the city, it had traveled farther and farther into the hills—and he'd had more and more trouble following it inconspicuously.

The van was intended as the Hardys' mobile base of operations. Frank had crammed it with state-of-the-art surveillance and communications equipment, a portable crime lab, and a small but powerful computer. Joe had overhauled the van itself to prepare it for tough action at high speeds.

But now the van crawled along, trying to stay within sight but just out of view of the rickety old bus ahead. Joe clenched his teeth in frustration. *Make a run for it,* he urged silently. *Make your move! I want some action!* At this leisurely pace, it was hard to remember the real danger facing Frank.

At first, Joe didn't hear the tires grinding the road behind him. The long drive had dulled his senses. Then his eye caught sight of the car growing larger in his rearview mirror, and his muscles tensed for action.

He glanced at the mirror on the other door. An identical car was coming around his far side. Alert, he took in every sight and sound, calculating the danger.

Something didn't add up. Something was wrong.

Ahead, the bus had stopped, and the passengers were getting off. At that distance, he couldn't tell which of them was Frank, but there didn't seem to be any trouble. The Rajah's followers milled around the bus, stretching, getting some air. But the cars were even with him now, speeding to pass him.

"Pull over!" the driver to his left shouted. It was a cultist, and the pure white of his clothes clashed sharply with the cold black metal of the Smith & Wesson Magnum .38 on the seat next to him. The driver of the other car waved an Uzi submachine gun in the air. "Pull over!" he also cried. "Get out!"

Joe smiled. A flip of the switch, and shields would cover the windows, making the black van bulletproof. Then it would be easy to run the two cars off the road. He knew they were no threat to him, as long as he stayed inside. Once he left the safety of the van, though, his chances of survival would plunge.

But there was Frank to consider. If I show these guys what I can do, it could blow Frank's cover, Joe thought. Maybe I can bluff them.

He fingered the shield switch, and then, as the cars moved in front of him to block the road, he hit another switch instead. Gears ground, circuits clicked and whirred, and paneling slid down from the ceiling to cover the sophisticated electronics within the van. By the time Joe stopped at the side of the road, the inside of the van looked the same as any other customized van owned by half the teenagers in America.

The Rajah's gunmen, their weapons aimed at Joe, bolted from their cars, ran to the van, and flung its doors open.

"Hey, dude," Joe mumbled. He smiled stupidly at the gunman. "What's happenin'? Rad day for a ride, isn't it? I mean, like, totally awesome."

"Shut up," the man with the Magnum ordered. He clamped a hand around Joe's neck and yanked him from the driver's seat. Joe landed on the road—hard.

The pain maddened him. His eyes flared with anger, and, instinctively, he clenched his fists and started to rise to fight his attacker. Then he remembered Frank. Neither gunman had seen his reaction or how ready for a fight Joe was, and for

20

his brother's sake, he choked back his anger. But if the chance came to use it, he would gladly let it out.

The man with the Uzi poked his head into the van and looked around. "Nothing here," he said. "Looks like he's just some kid, out on a joy ride."

"I don't believe that," the other gunman replied grimly. Squinting his tiny, dark eyes into pinpoints, he glared at Joe. "He's hiding something."

He seized Joe under the arm and hauled him to his feet. Jutting his hand out sharply, he knocked Joe back against the van and lifted the Magnum so that its muzzle was an inch from Joe's nose. "What are you hiding, kid? Why are you following the bus? You've got about thirty seconds to spill your guts before I do it for you."

The other gunman looked on in horror. "You crazy, Bobby? He's nobody! Let him go!"

"Look at him!" the one called Bobby cried. "He's not afraid. He's not even sweating. This guy's used to danger and plenty of it, and that makes him too dangerous to live."

Joe felt his jaw tightening. The anger was welling up inside him again. He tensed his muscles, waiting for the time to make his move.

"You're paranoid," the other gunman said. "We kill him, and it'll be trouble for everyone."

"I've got that figured," Bobby replied. "We get one of the kids—let's make it a girl—to claim he

21

tried to kidnap her. When it turns out he had a gun, the cops'll know we had to shoot him to defend her."

"I don't have a gun," Joe said calmly.

"When they find you, you will." Bobby's eyes bored deep into Joe's. "Is that a bit of fear I see there? Oh, I hope so. That's just how I want to remember you." His finger tightened on the trigger.

"Bobby, no!" screamed the man with the Uzi. Bobby turned his head and started to growl a response.

Joe's fist slammed up, ramming Bobby's gun hand aside. A shot roared into the air, and before Bobby knew what was happening, Joe grabbed his wrist. He spun the gunman as he forced his arm down, then twisted behind him and locked an elbow around Bobby's neck, pressing at his windpipe.

The gun was still in Bobby's hand, but Joe's hand was wrapped around the gunman's, forcing his arm to point in whichever direction Joe wanted. At the moment it was pointed directly at the man with the Uzi.

"Drop it," Joe said. "Maybe you can still get me, but you'll have to go through your pal to do it."

The man with the Uzi licked his lips anxiously and fingered his gun. Joe tightened his grip on Bobby, and Bobby let out a moan then collapsed unconscious in Joe's arms.

22

Long seconds ticked by. No one moved.

"Drop it and I'll let you live," Joe said. "That's a better deal than your pal would have given me. I'd rather not do anything we'll both regret, but I will if I have to, and then you might not be around to regret it.

"Drop it," he repeated softly.

The Uzi slid from the man's fingers and dropped into the dirt.

Joe pried the Magnum from Bobby's fingers and let him slide to the ground. Taking careful aim, he flagged the other gunman over to the van.

"You said you wouldn't kill me," the gunman whimpered. He glanced over first one shoulder and then the other, looking for somewhere to run, then finally staggered to the van, defeated.

"I just need you under wraps for a while," Joe said. "It'll be a little uncomfortable, but you'll be all right. Oh. There's just one other thing.

"Take off your clothes."

Frank's eyes opened wide at the sound of the shot, and his muscles tensed. Holly and the Rajah fled from his mind, and all he could think about was his brother, alone, facing an unknown enemy.

He could see nothing of what was happening behind the black van. He started to run, and all of a sudden found a half dozen of the Rajah's followers blocking his path. In their midst was Chandra.

"It's time to get back on the bus, Frank," she said. Her voice was calm but stern, her tone indicating she was used to being obeyed.

"But something's going on back there," Frank said. As soon as he was finished speaking, he clamped his mouth shut. What could he say? Rescuing his brother would blow his cover, but he had to find out what was happening. "There was a shot, wasn't there? Someone may be hurt."

Sighing, Chandra turned toward the black van. She cupped her hands around her mouth and called, "Is anyone injured back there?"

A figure in white stepped out from behind the van. "No," he shouted. "Some engine trouble, that's all. We'll have him out of here in no time." Then, almost as an afterthought, he added, "All praise to the Rajah."

"All praise to the Rajah," the cultists who milled around Frank chanted in unison. Then, single file, they climbed back aboard the bus.

Almost visibly, the resistance melted out of Frank's body, his sudden rebelliousness replaced by the gratefulness and meekness that had secured him a place as one of the Rajah's followers. He joined in line and suppressed the grin that threatened to form on his lips, just as he had swallowed the gasp that had almost escaped him moments before.

"You mustn't be so willful, Frank," Chandra said as the ride got under way again. "Willfulness is what brought you down in your previous life.

You must learn to control your own selfish desires and trust in the way of the Rajah."

"The Rajah is joy. The Rajah is peace. The Rajah loves us all," said a blond girl seated next to him. Frank nodded. Bowing his head and closing his eyes tightly, he repeated her chant.

But it was not those words that gave him a feeling of peace and warmth. It was others. In his head, he repeated the words of the white-garbed man who had yelled from the van. The words themselves were not important to him. He just wanted to hear them again and again, as best he could.

For the words and the clothes were those of a Rajah devotee, but the voice was that of Joe Hardy.

# Chapter

## 4

THE RAJAH'S COMMUNE had settled in a valley high in the Adirondack Mountains. Twin peaks guarded the valley, limiting travel to the one road that led into the commune.

Though the legend was persistent among the Rajah's followers that he had performed a miracle and created the valley himself, the land had been used for farming for three hundred years, and the cultists continued to farm the rich soil.

Once a month, some of them traveled halfway down one of the mountains, to the small town of Pickwee, to trade their crops for other supplies. For the most part, they grew all of their own food and made all of their own tools.

The Rajah had promised them a simple life, and what they did not have was considered unnecessary for that life. Even the housing was simple: a cluster of small log lodges, with the girls living in some of them and the boys living in the others. The lodges held only cots, with each lodge sleeping forty in tight quarters. No room for privacy, Frank thought. No room for individuality.

But obviously, privacy and individuality were unimportant to the Rajah's followers. Though they had nothing more than the clothes on their backs and a bed to sleep in at night, they were always laughing and smiling.

If doubt or curiosity existed in the commune, Frank could see no sign of it. The Rajah's followers were blissfully happy, happier than anyone Frank had ever known and happier than he'd ever thought anyone could be.

His first day at the commune was uneventful. As the bus pulled in, the members stopped what they were doing and ran to meet it. Frank stepped down into a cheering mob, and a flurry of hands clutched and shook his, patting him on the shoulders and back, welcoming him.

As others came off the bus, the crowd turned its attention to them. Only one boy stayed with Frank. He was sixteen at most, and though his flaming red hair recently had been cut short, it was starting to curl again as it grew out. His hair color and the many freckles that dotted his beaming face marked him as Irish-American.

Despite Frank's attempts to walk away from

him, the boy kept pace, never breaking his smile for a moment and constantly staring into Frank's eyes.

"Frank, this is Kadji," Chandra said after a few moments. "He'll be your companion while you're here."

Frank opened his mouth in surprise. "But I thought you—"

Chandra cut him off. "I must return to the city, to give peace to other poor, lost souls. Kadji will help you find your place in the commune. He will always be here for you, and he will give you any help you need. Goodbye, Frank."

With that, Chandra turned and climbed aboard the bus. The motor started, and the bus rattled through the gate, to begin its long journey back to the city.

"Don't worry, Frank," Kadji said cheerfully. "I remember how I felt when I first arrived. When the bus left, I was scared that I'd be trapped here. But I like it here, and so will you."

"She said I could leave if I wanted to. And I thought she *liked* me . . ."

Kadji nodded. "She loves you, Frank. We all love you, and we all love each other, in a pure and spiritual way. Anyway, if you still want to, you'll be able to leave when the bus gets back. In a few days . . ."

Frank gazed around the compound, trying to

look relaxed and fascinated. In reality, he was remembering every detail and studying every face.

The sleeping lodges seemed scattered at first, but as Frank walked around, he realized that they were set up to look as if they were all radiating from a large, old farmhouse. Though rustic, it had obviously been remodeled recently, with one-way windows and high security locks on the doors.

"Who lives there?" Frank asked.

"That is his home," Kadji replied. The smile faded from his lips, and he cast his eyes down and lowered his voice to a whisper. "I am not worthy to speak his name."

The Rajah, Frank mused. Cultists passed him, two by two, always a girl with a girl or a boy with a boy, but none of them went near the house. He scanned their faces.

Holly Strand was not among them.

"Does he ever come out?" Frank asked. "Do you ever see him?"

"He appears, though his holiness is sometimes too much to look upon." Kadji was barely breathing by then, and in between sentences, his lips moved wordlessly in prayer. "During the festival. During the name giving."

"During what?"

"The festival when you will become one of us. He will give you your new name."

"Like Kadji?" Frank asked. "What's your real name?"

Kadji raised his head, smiling peacefully again. "My real name is Kadji. I had another name once, but that was my name in sin. It's dead and forgotten, like my old life."

Uh-huh, Frank thought. "The people I see," he said, "are they everyone who lives here, Kadji? I thought the place was much bigger."

"Only some are here," Kadji replied. "A few who have fully developed spirits are allowed to return to the outside world. Chandra was one of those. Some work in the fields, gathering crops. Some cook, some clean, and some wash clothing. Some are off playing games."

"Do they ever . . ." He wasn't sure how to ask without arousing Kadji's suspicions. But he's expecting me to be suspicious, Frank reasoned. I can ask anything, as long as I don't seem to be looking for something specific. He'll just try to ease my mind. "Does everyone ever get together at one time?"

"At the name giving," Kadji said. He stared deep into Frank's eyes again, smiling his placid, blank smile. "Everyone will come to greet you, Frank. Everyone wants to be your friend. You'll see."

He pointed across the yard, to an area where the field had been partly cleared away. A pole was stuck in the ground there, and a ball hung from a rope attached to the top of the pole. Several of the Rajah's followers were congregating around the pole.

"There's a tetherball game starting up, Frank," Kadji said, with controlled excitement in his voice. "Do you like to play?"

"Sure," Frank said.

"Oh, good! Let's get in on the game." He grabbed Frank by the elbow and pulled him toward the pole. "This will be fun. You'll like it here, Frank. You really will."

Breaking into a light jog, to hurry to the game, Frank smiled at Kadji and said, "You know, I really think I will."

I'll wait a few hours, and then tell them that I want to stay. They'll bring everyone together for the name giving, Frank thought.

And that's where I'll find Holly.

On the other side of the one-way windows, a dark-eyed man watched as the recruits left the bus. He was taller than Frank and muscular as well, and he was dressed in a tunic and slacks like the cultists, but his clothes were made of the finest purple silk. His face was narrow and bearded, with a strong Roman nose, and his heavy brows shadowed his eyes, giving him an air of mystery and power.

He was the Rajah.

"Him," said a girl's voice. She was partly

hidden in the shadows of the house, but her delicate hand was visible in the light from the window as she pointed at the bus.

The Rajah looked out at Frank Hardy, who was surrounded by the cheerful cultists. "You know him?"

Holly Strand stepped out of the shadows. Her long auburn hair fell freely down her back, and her slender face was marred only by the sadness in her eyes. "His name is Frank Hardy," she said emotionlessly. "I grew up with him. His father's a detective or something."

The Rajah stroked his chin. "The one who came around, asking questions about you, yes. And now his son . . ."

Suddenly he swept Holly into his arms and held her close, pressing her head against his chest. His reddish brown beard blended into Holly's hair, the two colors matching perfectly. His eyes were raised upward, and tears formed at the edges of them. "Of all these, you are my favorite, Yami. All these have come to me, but you alone I sought."

"I know, Great Rajah. Thank you."

"Then, for what you are about to do, you are forgiven," he continued. "Go, and make sure he doesn't see you until the proper time." He released her, and she backed away, pressing her fingers against her tear-streaked cheeks.

"I don't want to go," she sobbed.

"Go," he said. "It is my will." He left the room, slamming the door behind him.

In the empty room, Holly Strand felt terribly alone. Since she had come to the commune, she had been free of the terrible emotions that had always confused and troubled her. Now they flooded back, and even though she fought them, she could feel the fear and doubt.

She clenched her fists until her fingernails left red marks on her palms. The effort steadied her. She knew she had no right to doubt the Rajah's plans, and now she was filled with horror at her own weakness.

Choking back her rage, she ran from the room and out of the house, letting the back door swing wide open. She knew she must go to her lodge and pray until the Rajah needed her.

Joe Hardy caught the door and slipped inside the Rajah's house before letting it close.

He was still amazed at the ease with which he had infiltrated the commune. Dressed as one of them, he had simply walked in across the fields. No one had batted an eye. He suspected that there was something about his outfit, taken from one of the men who attacked him on the road, that identified him as a member of the Rajah's special guard.

Joe grinned briefly as he thought about those two gunmen. He'd dumped them in the woods off the highway with their hands and feet loosely bound. Clothes do make—or unmake—the man, he thought.

Whatever the reason for the success of his disguise, no one had stopped or questioned him. After spotting Frank playing tetherball, he had briefly checked the lodges. There was nothing peculiar about them, he thought, except how people could stand to live in them. The farmhouse was the only building he hadn't checked, and for a few moments, the locks had stymied him.

Then the door had opened, and suddenly Joe was in.

The house was not what he expected. The room that the Rajah and Holly had stood in was bare, except for what looked like a small altar in one corner and kneeling mats on the floor. It was the Rajah's private temple, barren and austere.

But in the next, soundproofed room, Joe found a wide-screen television hooked up to a stereo videocassette recorder. A complete, state-of-the-art stereo system sat next to it. Records and videotapes were racked along an entire wall. In the middle of the room, with a good view of the TV screen and halfway between two six-foot-tall stereo speakers, was a reclining chair.

On the wall opposite the record racks was another door, leading to another room, and Joe could hear an excited voice shouting there. He put his ear against the door and listened.

"We've got a good thing going here!" the voice cried. "Why should we risk it on this fool scheme? Just throw him out. There's nothing anyone can do to us. You know that!"

"It is my will," a deep, soft voice replied. It was the Rajah. "Do not question my will."

"Boy, you're really getting into this godhead stuff, aren't you?" the first voice said. "If I hadn't found you and come up with this scam, you'd still be hustling fortunes at Fourth of July sideshows."

"You are wrong," the Rajah said calmly. "There was no life before the Rajah, and you have always been Vivasvat."

Vivasvat exhaled sharply. "Mikey, Mikey," he said. "Remember me? This is Shakey Leland you're talking to. Okay, so we don't kick the guy out. Let's just kill him and bury him in the woods someplace. Nobody knows he's here. Nobody'll know the difference."

Now the Rajah's voice grew enraged. "Get out!" he ordered. "The boy is a gift. He will soon do our bidding, and he is not to be harmed! Do not speak to me of murder."

"Oh, I'll leave," Vivasvat shouted. "But we take care of the kid my way, and don't you dare lecture me. You've murdered, too, Mikey. You can call it penance or justice or divine will if you want, but it's still murder. So spare me the piety!"

Suddenly the door opened, and Joe and Vivas-

35

vat stood face-to-face. Vivasvat's lips curled with rage, and he aimed a pistol at Joe. Desperately, Joe grabbed for his own gun, the Magnum he had taken from Bobby, but Vivasvat jabbed his hand upward. The pistol butt smashed into Joe's jaw, and he crumpled to the floor.

# Chapter

## 5

THE HAZE PARTED slowly. Joe Hardy wanted to clear the mist from his eyes with a wave of his hand, but neither hand could move. He blinked instead, and the mist finally evaporated.

Joe lay on his stomach on the floor of the stereo room. His clothes were gone, and he shivered as the temperature in the valley dipped with the dusk.

Something scratched at his wrists, and he realized that his hands had been bound behind his back. A sandaled foot stood directly in his line of vision. The Rajah, cruel and majestic, was seated at the end of the room.

Vivasvat reached down, grabbed Joe by the hair, and lifted his head so that their eyes met. "You're Joe Hardy," he said. "Don't bother to deny it. We have your identification."

"Ask the young man why he is here," the Rajah commanded. "Does he intend to help his brother?"

Joe's mouth dropped open. He knows, he thought. He knows the whole plan. Joe shut his mouth and glared at the cult leader, uncertain of what to say.

The Rajah stood and strode across the room, standing so tall that his feet seemed not to touch the ground. "You don't want your brother to join us, do you?"

Joe sighed with relief and stifled a chuckle. "That's right," he said. "I came to get Frank out of here."

A grim smile came to the Rajah's lips, and Joe suddenly knew he had made a mistake. He could tell from the Rajah's satisfied expression that they hadn't known for sure if he and Frank were brothers. He had just confirmed it for them.

"What're we wasting time with this mook for?" Vivasvat said. "He's seen our operation. He knows about the security guards. I say we get rid of him."

"Enough," the Rajah commanded. "Send someone for the van he was driving, and bring it to the commune." To Joe, he said, "You have sinned against my law. The commune meets tonight to welcome your brother to our number— did I mention he has asked to join us?—and they shall decide your punishment."

"Great," Joe said.

"Shut up, creep." Vivasvat put his mouth next to Joe's ear and very softly continued, "Say anything to anyone about what you've heard here today, and I'll kill you on the spot. Got it?"

Joe nodded.

"They may decide to let you go," the Rajah said. "In any case, you won't be with us much longer." The Rajah left the room, laughing coldly.

She appeared in the doorway of the lodge, a thin silhouette framed against the growing bonfire outside. Frank stared at her, mystified by her sudden appearance, but Kadji's eyes bulged in horror.

"You can't come in here, Yami," Kadji croaked, his voice sticking in his throat. "Only men are allowed in the men's lodge."

"Then send Frank out," she said. "I want to see him before he . . . before he joins us."

Kadji shook his head fiercely. "I'm responsible for him. If anything happens—"

"It won't," she replied. "Please." She looked at Frank with mournful, lonely eyes. "Can't we please talk for a few minutes, Frank?"

Frank sat on the edge of his cot, staring at her. He had bathed in preparation for the festival and had just begun to dress when she appeared. "It's all right," he told Kadji. "I'll be back in time for the name giving." He slipped on a tunic.

"He's your responsibility, Yami," Kadji called bitterly as Frank reached the lodge door.

"Yours!" He was still muttering as Frank took Holly's hand, and they stepped into the cool mountain night.

"Do I call you Yami?" Frank asked after they had walked some distance.

The bonfires were far behind them, though Frank and Holly were still on commune land. Above them, the stars were clearer than Frank had ever seen them. There were hundreds, perhaps millions, more than could be seen from New York City or even from Bayport, because there were no other lights to blot them out. Frank felt as if he were walking under the very roof of heaven.

"Call me Holly," she answered. "I've waited so long to be called Holly again." She licked her lips, hesitant to speak. Finally she said, "I'm surprised to see you, Frank. You're the last person I'd expect to see in a place like this."

Frank chuckled. "Why? Didn't you think I wanted peace? Didn't you think I wanted somewhere to belong?"

"I always thought you had those things. You were so good at sports, and girls were always running after you."

"After me?" he asked skeptically. "I never noticed."

She wrinkled her nose at him. "No, you were so hooked on . . . what's her name? Callie Shaw?"

"Callie. Huh! She was always on my case. Do

this, do that. What a nag! Just like my old man. Finally I couldn't take it anymore."

"So you left," she said. "I know that story. Still, I wish I'd gotten a fraction of the love and attention from my father that you got from yours."

They walked some more in silence, then she clutched his arm fiercely. "You've got to get out of here, Frank. You're in terrible, terrible danger."

"What do you mean?" he asked. There was a note of disbelief in his voice, but his mind was racing, calculating the options he'd have if he were discovered.

"It's the Rajah. He's cruel and ruthless. He takes perfectly sweet teenagers and twists them into merciless robots. He steals our minds, Frank. He steals our souls."

Frank looked at her intently for a moment. "If this place is so bad, why don't you leave?"

Holly bit her lip. "You don't understand. I know too much. If I go, they'll follow. They'll find me and kill me. I'm safe only here." She shuddered, and Frank took her in his arms.

"Shhh," he said, stroking her hair. "It's all right. No one's going to hurt you." She sobbed against his shoulder until no more tears would come.

"We'd better be getting back," Frank said.

But the next thing he knew, she had stood on tiptoes, wrapped her arms around his neck and was pulling his mouth to hers. Then she pulled away, her cheeks red with embarrassment.

In the distance, Frank could hear the happy chants of the cultists, but it seemed that he and Holly were the only people in the world, and everything else was a dream.

Holly looked at him anxiously. "Take me away, Frank. You can protect me."

He lowered his head. "We can't talk now. We'd better be getting back," he said, and the wind went out of her as if he had punched her in the stomach.

As they walked back to the huts, Holly asked, "If it hadn't been for Callie Shaw, would we have gotten together?"

"I can't answer that question," Frank said carefully. She nodded and sighed, saying nothing else on the walk back.

It wasn't until they had reached the lodges that they noticed something had changed. When they'd left, a bonfire had been burning in front of each lodge. Now there was just one huge blaze in the midst of the lodges, in front of the Rajah's home.

"It's not a name giving," Holly said, the color draining from her cheeks. "It's an inquisition. Someone will face the test of the flames."

"The test of the flames?" Frank repeated. "What's that?"

"Someone has betrayed us," she replied, as if

she hadn't heard him. Then she glared at him with fear in her eyes. "I must go," she said. Before he could speak, she ran into the darkness.

Frank was puzzled. Holly had seemed so determined before, so anxious to be rescued. Then, when she saw the fire, awe and superstition had twisted her features into a mask of dread. It was as if she had become some other person.

Yami, thought Frank. The Rajah's Yami, as he named her. Is that what would happen to me if I stayed? If I wanted to stay? Is that what happens to all of them?

Slowly he entered his lodge. For the first time, all lights were turned out, and he was surprised that Kadji wasn't there waiting for him.

But something was there, waiting in the darkness. Frank couldn't see it in the gloom, but he felt its presence. It pressed against his chest, keeping him from inhaling. Nothing's there, he told himself, but terror welled up in him all the same. Nothing's there!

At the far end of the lodge, something moved toward him. Frank could only spot flashes of purple, glinting in the blackness. He tensed and backed away.

"Where are you going, boy?" said a familiar voice behind him. Frank looked over his shoulder at the grim face of Vivasvat.

"You and the girl, Yami," said the Rajah as he stepped into the faint light from the bonfire outside. Vivasvat caught Frank's arms in an iron grip and pinned them to his side. "Did you touch?" the Rajah asked.

"No," Frank said. "Your will—"

"Good," the Rajah interjected. He smiled slightly. "You were gone for some time. What did you discuss?"

"We . . ." Frank began. He thought for a moment. "Holly . . . Yami hates it here. She asked me to help her escape," Frank said.

"And will you?" the Rajah asked.

"She is misguided," Frank replied solemnly. "I came here for peace. I want you to teach me the way of peace, Master."

A cold chuckle burst from the Rajah's lips. "Very good, boy. You have taken your second step toward peace, forgoing temptation and speaking the truth."

Frank gasped. "You knew?"

"It was my will. All things are my will here." The Rajah stepped past Frank and Vivasvat and into the night, gesturing for them to follow. Vivasvat let go of Frank's arms.

"You may serve me again tonight," the Rajah said to Frank, who was following a step behind. Vivasvat hung back, staying away from them. "We have had an intruder, a devil who came to do evil. Tonight you must hold the torch of truth to him, to burn out his lies and release him to glory."

"I don't understand," Frank said.

"He will be tested with flames. They will not burn the holy, but all evil things fear them. You shall hold the first torch, boy, and then I will give you your name."

Frank's mouth and throat went dry as they turned a corner. The Rajah's followers were gathered around the bonfire, each holding a torch. They stared savagely at a pole in front of the Rajah's home. A boy was tied to it—the boy who was to face the flames.

The boy was Joe Hardy.

# Chapter
## 6

THE RAJAH STOOD before his followers and raised his hands in benediction. "Bless you, my children," he said. They had been chanting loudly, but the chanting dropped to a whisper when he spoke, and they turned their eyes to the ground. Only Frank kept his eyes on the Rajah as he desperately tried to think of a plan.

"Brothers! Sisters!" the Rajah went on. He swung an arm down, pointing a long, bony finger at Joe. "We have a devil in our midst!" A hush like a breath of air passed through the crowd.

"He comes to destroy our faith! A soul has come to us for salvation, and this devil comes to drag that soul back to the world of evil!" The cultists howled in outrage, flinging curses at Joe. "But his victim shall be his savior instead! Step up, Frank Hardy—you who will be called Vaisravana—and prove yourself worthy."

"Vais-ra-va-na, Vais-ra-va-na," the cultists chanted over and over. The Rajah stepped among them and pulled a stick of wood from the bonfire. Flames crackled at one end of the stick as the Rajah held it out to Frank.

"Take it, Vaisravana," the Rajah said. "Take it, and burn the devil from your brother! My will is your will! My will is your will!"

"His will is your will," the Rajah's followers intoned. Frank looked at them, and as he watched, their faces began to change.

They know what's coming, he thought, and the knowledge sickened him. They were all children, really, from homes like his and like Holly's, but he could tell by the look in their eyes that they wanted to see blood. They played at being holy, but the ritual and the Rajah had released something in them that only blood would satisfy.

He wanted to run, but there was nowhere he could run to.

With trembling fingers, he took the fiery brand.

Vivasvat clapped his hands, and a dozen men emerged from the throng. They formed a human corridor from Frank to Joe and stood there, legs spread and arms folded, staring at Frank. All around, he could hear dozens of voices blending into one, speaking a single word in endless repetition. "Vais-ra-va-na, Vais-ra-va-na!"

Quietly the Rajah said, "Do it."

The brand had burned down, and flames licked at Frank's hand as he moved toward Joe. He didn't notice the heat.

Frank studied the faces as he passed the rows of men who, though they wore the same garb as the Rajah's followers, were older than most of them. The faces were hard and merciless, and beneath each tunic showed the telltale bulge of hidden pistols. The Rajah's bodyguards.

If I could just get to a gun, Frank thought.

He had no more time to think. He was standing before Joe. Every eye was on them. The chanting had become a shriek, the only sound in the world. From the corner of his eye, he could see the bodyguards fingering their guns, and the Rajah was grinning mirthlessly and nodding. The chanting went on and on.

Mouthing a silent prayer, Frank thrust the firebrand at Joe.

Suddenly he spun, hurling the wood at the bodyguard standing to his left. The man screamed as the flames brushed him, and jumped back. For a moment, everyone watched him, and Frank leaped in the air. He smashed out with his foot at the bodyguard to his right, striking him in the stomach. The guard doubled over.

Frank caught the man in midfall and flipped him around. The bodyguard slammed against the ground. In a flash, Frank reached into the man's tunic. Out came a .357 Magnum, and Frank fired it once in the air. The chanting stopped.

Frank backed around the pole, keeping the gun trained on the Rajah. "Stay back," he warned. "Anyone so much as breathes hard and your leader gets it." To Joe, he said, "You okay?"

"A little bruised, but otherwise pretty good," Joe replied. "Too good to hang around with these creeps any longer. Ready to go?"

"As soon as I get you untied," Frank said. He tried to loosen the knot at Joe's wrists, but he couldn't afford to look at the rope. If he took his eyes off the Rajah, even for a second, or if he moved the gun slightly, it would be all over.

Frank didn't mind fighting the bodyguards if it came to that, but he couldn't face the prospect of fighting the cult. Despite what he had seen in their eyes moments before, they were only frightened innocents at heart.

Keeping his eyes riveted on the Rajah, Frank whispered into Joe's ear, "As soon as I shoot, run for the van. Understand?"

"But I'm still tied," Joe whispered back. "How—?"

"Just do it," Frank murmured. Then, to the Rajah, he shouted, "Come here! Now!"

The Rajah stood still, his mouth dangling slightly open. His lower lip trembled, and there was, at last, fear in his eyes. Are his followers looking at him? Frank wondered, though he dared not turn his head to check. Can they see that he's only a man, and a rotten excuse for a man at that?

"Come here," Frank repeated. "Don't make me kill you."

The Rajah walked forward, through the corridor of bodyguards. His eyes shifted left, then right, then left again, but there was no escape. No way he could push his men aside before Frank fired.

"Do not—" the Rajah started to say and then paused. His confident smile locked back into place, and he spoke steadily. "Do what you want with me, devil, but do not harm these holy souls." He spread his arms out, waving at his followers, and continued walking toward Frank.

He's good, Frank thought. He's really good. A true showman, even in the face of death. Then a terrifying thought hit him. What if he knows? What if he figured out I wouldn't gun down an unarmed man? That all this is an act?

No, he assured himself. If he knew that, Joe and I would be prisoners by now. Or worse.

When they were less than an arm's length apart, Frank grabbed the Rajah by the shoulder, spun him around, and wrapped an arm around the Rajah's throat. But as he did so, he lowered his gun. As one, the Rajah's followers lunged.

Frank fired his gun once. The Rajah stiffened and his eyes bulged, and Frank pushed the Rajah's slumping body away as the man fainted at the roar of the shot. The bullet ripped through Joe's ropes. Joe was free.

"Go!" Frank screamed and fired a round of shots over the heads of the crowd. The Rajah's bodyguards scrambled for cover, fumbling for their guns, and the cultists shrieked and scattered among the lodges.

Joe dashed for the black van. Oddly, no one barred his way. I guess they just weren't expecting us to make a break for it, he thought. The Joe Hardy luck, it seemed, was holding up. He reached for the door handle on the van.

The door burst open, smashing into Joe and knocking him off his feet. Dazed, he shook his head to clear the pain, and dimly he saw a man stepping out of the truck.

"Vivasvat," Joe said. "I thought I'd have to leave without getting another crack at you."

"You aren't going anywhere, boy," Vivasvat said. He crooked a finger at Joe and motioned him forward, challenging him. "Come on, boy. Let's see what you've got."

Joe vaulted up, head first, and butted Vivasvat in the stomach. Though the wind was knocked out of him, Vivasvat grabbed Joe by the ears and swiftly jabbed his knee up, smashing Joe in the Adam's apple. Joe staggered back, barely remaining on his feet.

"Come on, boy," Vivasvat taunted. "Come on."

Joe moved cautiously, his hands clenched into

fists and his left arm raised for protection. "Come on," Vivasvat repeated, and he laughed. Joe feinted with his left hand. Vivasvat knocked the hand aside, but in doing so opened himself up to Joe's right. Joe swung, putting all his strength behind the jab.

With a chuckle, Vivasvat stepped aside. Caught off balance, Joe lurched forward, and Vivasvat cupped his hands together and smashed them against the back of Joe's head. His knees weak, Joe staggered toward the black van.

In the corner of his eye, Joe saw Vivasvat coming up behind him. But he was still stunned. Vivasvat's blows were expertly placed, and though Joe was a fine amateur boxer, he could see he was outclassed by the Rajah's henchman.

Vivasvat swung again, and Joe brought both arms up in front of his face, fending off the blow. He fell back against the side of the van. Rest, he said to himself. Concentrate. Let him tire himself out and wait for the right moment.

A fist slammed against his temple, and another on his chest. A third blow smashed into his arms, and he felt the strength drain from them. They were useless now, dangling by his side.

Vivasvat smiled and put a hand under Joe's chin, steadying his head. "There," Vivasvat said. "That's just the way I want to remember you, wimp." He drew back a fist, aiming the killing blow at Joe's face.

As Vivasvat swung, Joe suddenly jerked his

head to one side. Vivasvat screamed, and Joe heard bones crunch against the tempered steel side of the van. He swung a right uppercut into Vivasvat's stomach, and the man doubled over. Joe slammed both hands down on Vivasvat's neck, and Vivasvat dropped to the ground and lay still.

Taking a deep breath, Joe climbed into the van and started the motor. He was too tired to hear the screams of the Rajah's followers or the gun battle going on between Frank and the Rajah's bodyguards. He switched on the lights and drove the van onto the battlefield.

"Over here!" Frank shouted, and Joe saw him huddled against one of the lodges. Bullets smacked into the van, but they had no more effect than Vivasvat's hand had. Joe drove the van to the lodge and hit a switch on the dashboard. The back door of the van swung open, and Frank leaped in.

"Let's get out of here," he said.

"What about Holly?" Joe asked. "We can't leave without her."

"We can't take her," Frank said with a sigh. "She tried to trap me for the Rajah. She doesn't want to go, and if we take her against her will, it's kidnapping. Let's go."

More shots were fired as the black van pulled away, and Frank stared out the back window. The Rajah's followers were coming out of hiding, screaming at the van and cursing. At the forefront of the mob was Holly. Frank could barely hear her above the din.

"I want to go, too!" she was yelling. "Take me with you, Frank! I want to go, too!"

"Stop!" Frank cried. "Back it up! She wants to be rescued."

"All right!" Joe said. He slammed on the brakes and spun the van around. They sped back the way they had come.

Shrieking, the Rajah's followers hurled themselves out of the way. Only Holly stood in their path, illuminated by the headlights and swaying slightly, tensing for action. As they zoomed past, Frank threw open the side door. His hand went out and locked onto Holly's wrist, and she was pulled from her feet and into the van.

"We did it!" Frank exclaimed as he slammed the door shut. "Let's go." The van roared into the night, followed only by slugs from the guns of the Rajah's followers.

In the grass next to the Rajah's home, Vivasvat nursed his broken hand. He sat there, crying, until a shadow fell over him. The Rajah stood there, a curiously self-assured expression on his face.

"This is your fault," Vivasvat said. "If you had let me handle it—"

"Everything that has been done has been my will," the Rajah said. Serenely he drew a pistol from his tunic. It was the same pistol Joe had carried when he entered the camp.

"I have no need of you anymore, my friend," said the Rajah, looking down. "Now that Strand is within my grasp, I am afraid we must say goodbye."

The Rajah fired six times, and each time, Vivasvat jerked. When the last shot was fired, Vivasvat fell on his back, his mouth and eyes open. The Rajah tapped the body twice, but there was no response. He went into his home, shut and locked the door, and dialed the phone. After a dozen rings, someone on the other end answered.

"Pickwee police?" the Rajah said in a grieved tone. "This is the Rajah. I regret to say that my commune has been invaded. One of my charges was kidnapped, and my assistant was murdered. . . . What? Yes, the murderer left his weapon here. I'm sure his fingerprints are all over it.

"His name? I only heard it once. But I believe he called himself Joe Hardy."

# Chapter

## 7

"NO ONE'S FOLLOWING US," Frank said. He gazed out the back window of the black van, but only the gravel road and silent forest showed in the red glare of the taillights. Beyond that was nothing but darkness.

Clouds had moved into the area, blotting out the moon and stars. If anyone was following them, they were doing it without lights, severely limiting the chances of catching up. Aside from dull thunder in the distance, the only sound was the ricochet of gravel off the van's underbelly as it sped down the mountain.

"No readings on the sensors," Joe said, glancing at the readout from their surveillance equipment as he drove. "There's no one within half a mile of us, if the infrared scopes aren't on the fritz. We did it!"

"That was some stunt you pulled, brother, going in there in disguise," Frank replied. "Why didn't you stick to the plan?"

"Sometimes you have to play these things by ear," Joe said, laughing. "Go with whatever works, that's what I say."

"It didn't work," Holly said, in a voice so low it could barely be heard. Both Hardys raised their eyebrows in surprise. Those were the first words Holly had spoken since they'd left the commune, but she wasn't making any sense.

"Shhh," Frank said comfortingly. "You're safe now, Holly. No one's going to hurt you anymore."

"No, you're wrong," she said. She sat back against the wall and drew her knees up until they pressed against her chin. She wrapped her arms around her legs, and fatigue and fear reddened her eyes. "You're wrong about everything. The Rajah hasn't let us go. He's toying with us. I know he is. Just like I know my father sent you."

Frank shook his head. "It's not true. He doesn't know we're here, and neither does our dad. We came here because you needed help and we could give it. And you don't have to worry about the Rajah, either."

"Yeah, you make too big a deal about him," Joe said. "He's not so tough."

"You don't know anything about him," Holly snapped. "He'll catch me, and he'll take me back, and he'll destroy you. I should never have left the commune."

Joe smirked, though he made sure to keep his face turned away from Holly. She's nuts, he thought. That creep's got his followers so wound up they think he can do anything.

"I'll tell you what, Holly. There's a village a little ways down the mountain, called Pickwee. We'll get in touch with the police there and have them escort you home. Then the Rajah won't be able to get his hooks into you again."

She winced at the mention of home and un-curled her body, shivering. "Hold me, Frank," she said, and he put his arm around her shoulder. She rested her head on his chest and sighed.

"I don't want to go home," she declared. "I don't ever want to see my father again. Just let me stay with you, Frank."

Frank's mouth dropped open. For once, he didn't know what to say. In the driver's seat, Joe grinned, and the black van continued down the mountain.

The town of Pickwee had existed since the Revolutionary War. Originally one of the few coach stops in the Appalachians, it had become the home of a number of shops that served the farmers in the mountains. As a result, the town closed up when the sun went down, with only a bar and a gas station staying open late in the evening.

Joe pulled the van into the gas station and up to a pump. No one was around, and if not for a light on in the office, he would have thought the station was closed. He tapped the car horn twice, but there were still no signs of life.

Finally, after Joe had climbed out of the truck and started pumping gas himself, a dark-haired man in a checked shirt and blue jeans sauntered out from behind the station.

"What's your hurry, young fellow?" he asked Joe.

Inside the van, Frank heard the man. Holly had fallen asleep, using his chest as a pillow. Carefully he slipped out from under her, cradling her head in his hands. He lowered her head to the floor, and when he stepped out of the back door, she still slept peacefully.

She looked angelic, a child, but Frank couldn't think of her as a child anymore. She was warm and soft, and . . . He rubbed his eyes and tried to think of Callie, but her face kept blending in his mind with the face of Holly Strand.

Frank shut the back door and locked it. The station owner looked at him, then at Joe, then back at Frank, and he stepped back, suddenly wary.

"I ain't got no money, if you're thinking of robbing me," the station owner said. "You kids ain't looking for trouble, are you?"

"We're looking for a policeman," Frank said. "Any idea where the police station is?"

59

"Heck, that's closed this time of night," the manager replied. "Don't need it much up here. Sheriff Keller, he'd be in the bar by now. A fellow just ran over there with a message for him, matter of fact."

"Thanks," Frank said. He looked around. The bar was a block away, a brick building with tiny windows and a flashing neon sign in front of it. "Cruise on over and wait for me when you're done filling up, Joe."

Joe nodded.

As he neared the bar, Frank heard shouting. There was also muffled music, the sound of a jukebox turned low. Through the window, Frank could see a burly, bearded man pacing back and forth. He was screaming at no one in particular, and his long blond hair bobbed up and down as he walked.

His back had been turned when Frank entered, and before he noticed, Frank slipped around him and up to the bar.

"Don't worry about him," the bartender said to Frank. Like the screaming man, the bartender had a beard, though his was dark and crinkly. Between his teeth was a toothpick, and he leaned against the bar, leafing through a magazine. "That's Hobart. He's harmless, unless you step on his toes or try to steal his stuff. What can I get you?"

"I'm not old enough to drink," Frank said. "I'm looking for Sheriff Keller."

"You came to the right place," the bartender said. "Sheriff Keller's the coffee guzzler in back." He pointed to a row of booths along the back of the barroom. In one of the booths sat two men dressed in police uniforms. The older, who must have been fifty, had graying hair and a wiry mustache. Keller, Frank guessed. He wore no tie, his collar was unbuttoned, and he wrapped his hands around a cup of coffee and drowsily listened to the younger man.

The second man looked barely older than Frank, and unlike the older man, he wore a strictly regulation uniform. Even his badge looked freshly polished. He was waving his hands and talking excitedly, though he was making a point of keeping his voice down.

Frank sauntered over to the booth, but he froze as he heard what the younger policeman was saying: ". . . murder at the hippie camp up there, Sheriff. Couple of fellows burst in with this black van and grabbed a girl. Shot one of their high muckamucks on the way out. S'posed to be heading this way."

"I don't guess you got any names to go with all these stories?" Keller asked. He looked tired and impatient with the younger man, but Frank could tell from his tone of voice that he was getting interested in the case.

The younger man pulled a sheaf of notepaper from his pocket and thumbed through it. "Yeah, it was . . . Joe something or other . . ." He searched the last sheet of paper without luck. "I must've left it back at the station."

He rose from the booth and ran out the door. Frank breathed a sigh of relief when he saw the policeman heading away from the filling station and the van parked there. He was about to leave the bar himself when Keller glanced at him and barked, "You're a little young to be in here, aren't you? Let's see a card."

"I just came in for information," Frank said.

"Card!" Keller barked, and held out his hand. Frank dug his identification from his wallet and dropped it in Keller's palm. "Frank Hardy, huh? Had some private dick named Hardy nosing around here a couple weeks ago. He just wanted information, too. Know him?"

"Nope," Frank lied. He stepped around the booth so he could look out the door of the bar at the gas station. Joe was just pulling the van away. "Just a coincidence, I guess."

"Uh-huh," the policeman said, and gave Frank's identification back. "Just what kind of information do you want?"

"Some friends of mine told me there was a shortcut to Albany around here, but I got lost. Do you have any idea where I'd pick it up?"

Keller cracked his knuckles. "Quickest way to Albany is the Interstate. You're quite a ways off the track."

"I guess they were pulling my leg," Frank said.

"I guess they were," Keller sneered. "By the way, you wouldn't happen to have seen a black van in your travels, would you?"

Frank chewed on his lip as if he were deep in thought. After a couple of seconds, he replied, "Nope. Sorry." The policeman just stared at him and tried to crack his knuckles again, but no sound came.

"Well, I'd better be going," Frank said. The policeman nodded solemnly. "Thanks for your help," Frank called back as he reached the door of the bar. Keller still watched and absentmindedly picked up the coffee cup again.

The black van was parked outside, and Joe stood alongside it, leaning against the driver's door. When he saw Frank, he called, "So where's the help?"

Frank clamped a hand over his brother's mouth. "Keep your voice down," he said. "You're in a lot of trouble."

Joe stared in amazement as Frank pulled his hand away. "Me? What did I do?" he whispered.

"Someone got killed at the commune tonight," Frank growled. "The Rajah must have called the cops, because they're looking for a guy named Joe who's driving a black van.

"By now, every cop in the state will be looking for us. We've got to dump the van."

"I'll wake Holly," Joe said. "You heard what she said. If it wasn't for you, she'd be back with the Rajah right now. We can't get caught before we get her home."

Behind them, there was the sharp click of a revolver being cocked. The Hardys turned slowly to see Keller leveling a gun at them.

"Consider yourselves caught, boys," the policeman said. "Justice may be blind, but I ain't."

# Chapter

# 8

"YOU'VE GOT THE situation all wrong, Sheriff," Frank began. "We didn't—"

"Shut up," Keller barked. "Don't matter to me what the situation is. All I know is that the fellow up the hill pays me a lot of money to keep trouble away from him." His lip curled, exposing nicotine-stained teeth. "And you boys are trouble."

Joe clenched his fists. He took a step toward Keller. Keller aimed his gun at Joe's nose.

"Tough guy, huh?" Keller said. "Come on. I dare you. Come on!"

"No, Joe," Frank said calmly. Joe shook with anger for a moment, then his hands fell open. He backed away.

Keller waved them to the back of the van with his gun. "This where you've got the girl? Did you really think you could get her down this hill without getting caught?"

"Listen," Joe said, "you've got to see that she gets back to her father. It's important."

Keller snickered. "She's going back up the hill, boys. Where she belongs. If her daddy wants her, he'd better go up there and ask real nice." He grabbed the back door handle and turned it, releasing the catch.

The door slammed open, smashing into Keller. He toppled backward, spinning clumsily and trying to aim his revolver. Joe lunged at him, grabbing his wrist. The gun went off, spitting a bullet harmlessly into the ground.

Joe socked Keller. The sheriff toppled. He lay still on the ground.

"That awful man!" Holly cried, terror in her voice. "I've seen him at the commune. You can't let him take me back. You can't." Her voice disintegrated into choked sobs.

In houses and buildings all around, lights came on.

"Let's go," Frank said. "That shot must've woken the whole town. We'll never be able to explain beating up a cop, at least not in time to do Holly any good."

"Right," Joe replied. He jumped into the van past Holly, who was trying to catch her breath. As his fingers tapped the van's walls, paneling fell open to reveal hidden chambers.

From one, Joe snatched three insulated jackets, and from another a pair of survival knives. Finally, from the van's front panel, he disconnected the shortwave transmitter-receiver.

"What's going on?" Holly asked.

"Hey!" cried a voice from down the street. It was the deputy. "Hey!"

"We're going the rest of the way on foot," Frank said. He helped Holly out of the van, but warily kept his eye on the deputy, who was running toward them, drawing his gun as he neared.

"The Rajah pulled a fast one," Joe added. "We've got to ditch the van or it's all over." He tossed a jacket to Holly. "Put this on. It'll be a little big, but it's better than freezing to death."

He handed Frank a jacket and a knife. The deputy had almost reached them when his eyes fell on the prone form of the sheriff. With a gasp, he stopped dead in his tracks. "Sheriff Keller?" he said dumbly, as if awaiting a response.

Frank and Joe each grabbed one of Holly's arms and hurried her into the darkness. Alerted by the motion, the deputy raised his gun. He was too late. By then Frank, Joe, and Holly were fading into the shadows. The deputy leaped over the sheriff and ran around the van, then stared into the night.

The fugitives were gone, their trail marked only by a faint rustling of leaves that seemed to come from all around.

\*　　\*　　\*

Joe pushed aside a tree branch, holding it so that Holly could pass. Frank stayed several paces behind them, watching for signs of pursuit. The lights of Pickwee could be seen above them on the mountain, and more lights were turned on there by the minute.

But so far no one was on their trail. Frank was grateful for that much, at least, but he knew it was only a matter of time before Keller came to. Then the hunt for them would be on.

They had to find help.

But where? he wondered. He was sure they could make it down the mountain if luck stayed with them, but how could they get back to Bayport once they got to the highway? It would take days to get home on foot, and every minute they spent in the open increased their chances of getting caught. The highway patrol would certainly be looking for them.

Besides, Frank doubted that Holly could hold up. She was too fragile, a delicate flower. He just wanted to protect her, to keep her safe in his arms.

Frank snapped to attention, startled by that thought. He looked again over his shoulder, but the woods were still quiet except for the sound of Joe hacking away at the brush with his knife.

Holly marched behind Joe, easily keeping pace as if she were fresh and they were out for a jaunt and none of the day's events had happened. So, she had reservoirs of courage and strength after all, Frank realized. She was everything he could hope for.

Frank snapped to attention again. I'm falling in love with her, he thought. I really am. He found the thought oddly upsetting.

For what seemed like hours, the three continued through the woods and down the mountainside.

"What's that?" Holly asked, after they had walked several miles. She pointed through the trees.

Joe Hardy squinted. He could see nothing unusual in the endless swirl of bark and branches and leaves. There was nothing, he knew, except illusions caused by the moon reflecting off—

"What's the matter?" Frank asked as his brother stopped abruptly.

"The moon," Joe replied. "Moonlight's reflecting against something over there. Glass, I think."

They pushed through the brush, heading for the light.

The cabin they found was made of logs and plastered together with dried mud. It was half-hidden in the woods, in the smallest of clearings. There were no roads to it, and tree limbs blocked any view of it from the air. There was simply no way of telling it was there without stumbling on to it as they had done.

Frank crept up to the building, flattened himself against it, and craned his neck to peer through the window. Nothing moved inside the cabin. It housed a crude table and an old bed, both carved from logs, like the cabin itself. Dust carpeted the floor. There was no sign that anyone had been inside it for years.

"I think it's deserted," Frank said. "It's as good a place as any to stop and rest until sunrise."

Fear welled up in Holly's eyes again. "Those men," she said, her lips trembling. "They'll find us. They'll catch us."

"No, Frank's right," replied Joe. "We don't even know for sure if we're being followed. If we are, they're nowhere near us, and they could miss this cabin as easily as we almost did."

"If they haven't caught up with us by now, odds are we don't have to worry about them," Frank agreed. "It's what's ahead that we have to be prepared for."

Holly nodded, but there was still a hint of doubt in her slight smile. She tried the cabin door. It swung open at her touch.

"Go on in," Joe told Holly. "You'll be safe. We've got some things to do." She nodded again, then vanished into the cabin.

When she was out of sight, Joe unstrapped the communicator from his back, set it on the ground in front of him, and raised its antenna. Quickly he twisted the dial to a secret radio frequency and slipped in a special scrambler circuit. It was used only by members of the clandestine government agency called the Network.

"Hardys calling Gray Man," he said into his handset. "Hardys calling Gray Man. Come in, Gray Man. Mayday. Mayday."

White noise crackled unintelligibly on the speaker. Slowly a voice rose out of the static. "I read you, Hardy," it said.

It was the Gray Man.

Frank took the microphone as Joe fine-tuned the signal. "We've run into some trouble, Gray Man," Frank said. "We could use some backup."

"Negative," the Gray Man replied. "We are fully apprised of your situation. Until the charges against you have been dropped, this agency can't afford to become involved."

Joe took back the microphone. "We understand," he said. It was a lie. He didn't understand, but he knew there was nothing to be gained by challenging the Gray Man's decision. "At least send someone to Pickwee to get the van. We had to leave it there."

"Affirmative," the Gray Man's voice said. "Contact me again when it's over. And good luck." A loud click sounded, and white noise filled the airwaves.

Frank sighed. "Looks like we're on our own. Might as well leave the communicator here. It won't do us any good, and it'll only slow us down."

A scream ripped from the cabin.

71

"Holly!" Frank cried. Unsheathing his knife, he kicked in the cabin door. Holly was on the floor, crawling backward toward him. Her shrieks filled the air, but he couldn't see what she was shrieking at.

Then a creature with matted hair and mad eyes rose from the floor. It was giant, and in the darkness, it seemed like an ogre risen from the night. There had been no one in the cabin before, and no door except the one in front.

How did it get in? Frank wondered. He peered at the creature, and it became a bearded man who stood well over six feet tall. Long hair and a beard framed his face. In his hands was an ancient shotgun.

It was aimed at Frank.

# Chapter

## 9

FRANK'S BREATH CAUGHT in his throat. He had faced death many times before, and he would have thought its nearness could no longer affect him. But it did. Each time it came in some new form, equally dangerous and frightening.

The giant with the old gun was no exception. His matted, unkempt hair and his ragged clothes were laughable, but nothing was funny about the deadly weapon he held.

"Keep cool," Frank said. He raised his hands over his head. "We're not going to hurt you." As the giant approached, Frank slowly moved toward the near wall.

"My house," the giant said as they circled around each other. "You shouldn't be in Rosie's house."

"Rosie, huh? I bet you're named for your rosy personality," Frank quipped. He wished he were as confident as he sounded. Holly was curled up in the corner, trembling with fear. He couldn't depend on her in a fight.

The giant called Rosie steadied the gun. "Hold still," he growled.

Frank kept circling. He stopped finally at the back wall of the cabin. Rosie stood silhouetted against the window, his huge frame almost blocking out the moonlight.

"Think you're smart, don't you?" Rosie muttered. He peered with one eye down the shotgun barrel until Frank was locked in his sights. "This'll make you smart, smart boy."

He cocked back the shotgun's hammer with his thumb. His finger tightened around the trigger.

At that moment, Joe crashed through the window, smashing into Rosie's back. The giant tumbled forward and landed on his knees. His shotgun skidded across the floor and came to a halt at Frank's feet. Joe scrambled onto the giant and pinned him to the ground.

"You tricked me," Rosie muttered. Still stunned, he shook his head, and long strands of his hair whipped across Joe's chest. Bits of windowpane fell from his shoulders.

"Down, boy," Joe said as Rosie tried to stand. He shifted his weight onto the giant's shoulders to force him down again. To his surprise, Rosie didn't even seem to notice he was there, rising up stiffly, a growl forming in his throat.

Frank picked up the shotgun.

The giant lurched back suddenly, slamming Joe into the wall. The wind was knocked out of Joe, and he stumbled, his hand clutching at his chest.

Rosie's arm locked around his neck. The giant started to squeeze.

Frank took careful aim with the shotgun. "Drop him!" he shouted.

Rosie grinned savagely and tightened his grip on Joe's throat. "He hasn't got much time left." He squeezed again for emphasis. Joe sputtered and coughed. "Better give me the gun, boy. Otherwise . . ."

Frank was adamant. "Otherwise, I'll have to pull the trigger," he said calmly. "The second you kill him. Or you can let him go. Now."

The grin faded from Rosie's lips. He swallowed hard. Frank could see from the doubt in Rosie's eyes that he had gotten through to the giant.

They stood there for long seconds, staring each other down. Then Rosie opened his arm, and Joe fell away, gasping for breath.

Frank handed the shotgun back to the giant. "We didn't come here looking for trouble," he explained. "We only wanted shelter."

"Thought you was some of Keller's boys," Rosie said. Now that the fighting had stopped and he had his gun back, he smiled like they were all

75

old friends. "He sends them around now and then. He's been trying to drive me off the mountain since I got here."

Frank helped Holly to her feet. She was still cowering in the corner, her fear-glazed eyes fixed on the giant. "Shhh," Frank comforted her. "It was just a misunderstanding. Everything's all right."

Joe sat where he'd fallen, rubbing his neck. "We ran into the sheriff, too," he told Rosie. "He's enough to put anyone on edge. What are you doing all alone out here, anyway?"

"Surviving," Rosie replied. "See, someday our whole civilization's going to collapse. There won't be food in the cities, and it'll be every man for himself. I'm taking care of myself now, so I can make it through those times of woe."

"Really?" Joe said. "This is surviving?"

"It's all I need. Plenty of squirrels to eat, and some nuts and berries. It's easy when you get the hang of it. I raise a few crops, too, but Keller's boys keep tearing them up."

"How long have you been at this?" Joe asked.

Rosie opened his arms wide and beamed from one side of the cabin to the other. His chest heaved with pride. "I've had this little homestead since nineteen-seventy."

"They're here," Frank said abruptly. He was staring out a window at beams of light that pierced the darkness of the woods. Coming into the clearing were half a dozen men, led by Keller, who carried a hunting rifle and a bullhorn.

Rosie sidled up to the door. "Get away from here, Sheriff. I've got no business with you."

"Maybe I've got business with you," the sheriff replied. "We're looking for some kids—two boys and a girl. You seen them?"

"Can't say as I have, Sheriff," Rosie said.

"They're trying to surround us," Frank whispered as the six men fanned out around the edges of the clearing.

"Mind telling me how you broke your window, Rosie?" Keller called. "You're usually pretty careful about things like that."

Rosie spat out the door. "Maybe someone broke it for me, Sheriff. You'd know more about that than I would."

"There's no way we can make a run for it," Joe whispered. "We're trapped in here."

"Let's cut the chitchat, Rosie," the sheriff shouted. "We know you've got them in there. Send out the girl and we'll let the others go."

"Frank!" Holly pleaded. Rosie looked over at them, waiting for a response. Frank shook his head.

"Sorry, Sheriff," the giant said.

Keller's eyes bulged with anger. "I've been waiting years for this, Rosie. I never thought you'd give me an excuse to come down on you as hard as I wanted. But this time I got you."

Keller whipped his hand into the air. Rosie threw himself backward, out of the doorway.

A half-dozen explosions burst at once, sending chips of wood flying from the door frame. Frank pulled Holly to the ground to shield her from the shots, and Joe slid into the door, knocking it closed.

"Get over there," Rosie barked. He pointed to the trap door. "Start down. I'll catch up in a minute."

"You've got thirty seconds to come out," Keller yelled from outside. "Then we shoot the whole place down around you. We've got enough ammo to do it."

Frank dropped into the dark hole. His foot touched a ladder rung, slipped, and then he was tumbling. He managed to grab hold of the ladder. It seemed as if he was dangling over a vast, unending void, broken only by a soft hum.

There's an engine down here, he thought. Maybe Rosie's not so crazy, after all.

"Frank?" Holly said from somewhere in the darkness above him. "Where are you?"

"Here." He raised a hand, caught hers, and helped her down the ladder. He was suddenly conscious of her smooth fingers brushing and tightening against him. Then she was in his arms again.

"Watch out!" Joe called softly as his foot

kicked Frank's shoulder. "Coming through. Step aside."

A light glowed above them. "Take this," Rosie called. He dropped a flashlight into the shaft, and Joe caught it. "I'll be right—"

His words were cut off by bursts of gunfire followed by a dull thud.

"Rosie!" the three of them cried at once.

No answer came.

"They must have gotten him," Joe said over the gunshots. "All because of us." He turned sadly, swinging the flashlight up.

He jumped back, nearly knocking over Frank and Holly. A man stood before them, his long hair matted over his bearded, smiling face.

"I had to jump," Rosie explained. "That's bad. No time to latch the trap door. They'll find it as soon as they stop shooting." He took the flashlight from Joe and shone it into the darkness.

They were in a cave. Frank had been right about the motor. A small engine chugged and purred in a corner, and boxes filled with dried foods were stacked near it. Nearby were a small cot and a cooking stove. This was Rosie's real home, he realized. The cabin above was just for show.

Down a long corridor was a big-wheeler Jeep, the kind that was specially made for off-road travel.

Rosie ran for it, and the Hardys and Holly

followed. "Hop in," Rosie said. They scrambled aboard. It was old, they could tell, but in perfect shape. The engine started up as soon as Rosie turned the key.

"Ride out!" the giant cried, and the Jeep shot forward. Joe, Frank, and Holly screamed, and the Hardys both lunged for the steering wheel. Rosie laughed wildly, the look of madness creeping back into his face.

The Jeep careened straight at the cave wall.

# Chapter

## 10

IT WAS TOO late for Frank or Joe to move. The Jeep smashed head-on into the wall.

To their surprise, it kept moving. The wall had come down, and it was flapping on the front end of the Jeep.

Rosie chuckled. They had run through a canvas sheet that had covered the mouth of the cave. "I've had that up for years, to keep people from seeing where I live. From the outside, it looks just like a moss-covered rock." He laughed again. "Riding through it gets them every time."

"Them?" Joe said. "You've done this before?"

"Back during the Vietnam War, I'd drive draft dodgers to the Canadian border," Rosie replied. He stared wistfully at the sky. "We'd go all the way to the Saint Lawrence on back roads and off roads. A guy ran a speedboat out of Morristown into Canada. I wonder what ever happened to him. Those sure were the days."

He reached out the driver's window, grabbed the canvas, and pulled it back over the hood until it was all inside the car. The Jeep whipped between and around trees as if it were a dirt bike. It bounced over rocks and ditches. It was evident that nothing fazed Rosie, and he would stop for nothing.

"So what's your story?" Rosie asked. "Run a stoplight in Keller's county?"

"It's a little more complicated than that," Joe said. "We rescued Holly from a commune this evening."

Rosie cocked an eyebrow, and his face filled with a new respect for the Hardy boys. "The Rajah's spread, huh? Mean guys up there. They took some shots at me once just for hunting within a hundred feet of the place." He leaned over to Joe and winked. "I had to crack a few skulls over that one."

Then he straightened up, tilting his head back to talk to Frank and Holly. "How'd you get hooked up with that mob, missy?"

"You're mistaken," Holly said. She suddenly sounded cross. "The Rajah doesn't believe in guns. He'd throw anyone using them out of the commune."

"Wise up, Holly," Joe said in disgust. "Those

guys took shots at me, and someone killed Vivas-vat. They didn't do that with prayer."

"Joe," warned Frank.

"Get real, Frank," Joe shot back. "She sounds like she still believes in that creep."

"I don't!" she insisted. Tears welled up in her eyes. "I just want to go home! I just want to go home. . . ."

She buried her face in Frank's shoulder and sobbed. He slipped a comforting arm around her, softly smoothing her hair.

"Look what you've done," he scolded Joe. "Hasn't she been through enough?"

Joe scowled, but Rosie just grinned. If he had heard the conversation, he showed no sign of it. Steering the Jeep through the trees, he was lost in the fantasy world of his memories, dreaming of a life that had vanished more than a decade before.

"Thanks for getting us out of there, Rosie," Frank finally said. "I'm sorry you'll get into trouble for it."

"What?" Rosie drifted out of the daydream. "Oh, don't you worry about that. Keller never saw you in my place, and there's no evidence you were even there. If they shot up my cabin enough, I'll even get some money from the county out of this."

"How long before we hit the highway?" Joe asked.

Rosie laughed. "You don't know much about

being on the run, partner. The cops'll be all over the highway, waiting for you. You'll never get where you're going that way. You're getting out right about here."

Joe peered into the night. The woods had thinned into meadow, but they were still in the mountains. There were no signs of civilization there. "There's a road around here somewhere, right?" Joe asked.

"Nope," Rosie said. "Better." The Jeep screeched to a stop at the edge of a sloping cliff. "Look down there."

Joe climbed out of the Jeep and stared down the cliff. Far below was a rushing torrent of water—a river. But Rosie was wrong. It was too far below. There was no way to reach the river, and no way to travel on it if they did.

Rosie had led them to a dead end.

Frustrated, Joe kicked a stone down the cliff-side and listened to it roll. It hit something flat, bounced twice and rang as it bounced, then rolled the rest of the way and splashed into the water.

It rang! Joe thought excitedly. But it's stone. There's something else down there, something metal. He squinted. Partway down, almost hidden in the darkness, ran a set of train tracks.

"Where do they go?" Joe called.

The others left the Jeep and joined him. Holly's eyes widened in horror. "You don't expect us to walk back to Bayport, do you?"

"If you want, sure," Rosie said with a chuckle.

"Or we could wait for a train, couldn't we?" Frank said. "These would be cargo train tracks, since no passenger trains come through here. The train would slow down around this bend, to avoid throwing itself into the river. If it's going slowly enough, we should be able to hop on with ease."

He turned to Rosie, whose mouth dangled open with surprise. "That's why you brought us to this particular spot, isn't it?"

Rosie smiled cunningly. "You're pretty smart, all right. Except I bet you don't know when the next train's coming by."

"Nope," said Joe. "When?"

From the distance came a faint rumbling, and the ground began to quiver.

"In about two minutes," Rosie said, laughing.

"Come on!" Frank shouted, grabbing Holly's hand. "We've got to get down to the tracks. Quick!" They scrambled down the slope, sliding instead of staying on their feet. "Thanks again," Frank called to Rosie.

"Anytime, sport," Rosie called back. "If you're ever in these parts . . ."

His words were cut off by the roar of the train. It rumbled toward them, slowing as it hit the curve. They threw themselves against the hill as the train drew near.

Then it was passing them. Frank tried to yell orders, but the noise drowned his words. He strained his eyes, looking for the right boxcar to jump. Two cars filled with cattle passed, followed by cars full of coal and corn. Then he saw what he was looking for.

Coming up was an open, empty boxcar.

He grabbed Holly's wrist again and pulled her along. From the corner of his eye, he could see Joe on the move already, heading along the tracks the other way.

Nimbly Joe grabbed the handles on the side of the empty car as it eased past him. He was in his element, moving the way he had learned in the gym, pulling himself up the row of handles the way he would pull himself up a rope. It was child's play for him. With the grace of a trained gymnast, he swung from the handles through the open door. He was inside.

As the boxcar caught up to Frank and Holly and pulled past them, Joe held the frame of the door and stretched his arm out. Holly's fingers touched his and slid off.

"I can't do it!" she cried. "I can't! I can't!" She stopped, clenching her fists. She started to curl up like a child.

Frank clutched her around the waist and lifted her into the air. Without pausing to think, he tossed her bodily into the boxcar. She smacked the floor and rolled across it, dazed.

The boxcar moved on, leaving Frank running beside the train.

Joe howled and leaned out of the car again, hoping to give Frank a hold. It was no use. Frank stopped running and tried to catch his breath.

Throwing Holly aboard had used up the last of his strength. It was too long since he had slept.

Moments later, the last car in the train, a caboose, pulled alongside him. It's now or never, he thought, gritting his teeth. He took a deep breath and leaped. His hand caught the back steps of the train.

Gasping for breath, he pulled himself aboard and collapsed on the caboose's back platform. No one else was aboard the caboose. It was being used for storage, with big sacks of grain piled inside.

Frank leaned out over the edge of the platform and looked along the train. He could see Joe in the open car, smiling and waving. At last they were safe. They could rest.

A bullet splintered the wall above Frank's ear.

At the sound of the shot, loud even against the roar of the train, Joe leaped back to the door. Figures lined the hilltop they had just climbed down. Flames spat from their hands as the thunderclaps exploded.

It was Keller and his men. Rosie hadn't lost them after all, and they were shooting at Frank. The train rounded the mountain, allowing Joe a view of the back of the caboose. He could see his brother trying to stand and get a view of the shooters.

"No!" Joe cried.

A shot rang out, driving the figure on the caboose platform backward. It swayed on the opposite side for a second and then plunged off the train.

Joe scrambled to the other side of the boxcar and wrenched the door open. He saw the moon reflected in the water below. Next he saw a cloth-covered lump bob twice in the river, then sink beneath the swirling waters.

Frank was gone.

# Chapter
## 11

"HE WAS THE only one who loved me," Holly said through her tears.

Joe looked up wearily and shook himself awake. He sat crouched over his knees against the wall of the boxcar; he had been sitting that way for hours while Holly cried herself to sleep on and off.

"I don't want to talk about Frank anymore," he said. A lump about the size of a fist rose in his throat and choked him. He had always known that danger might one day take one of them. But not yet, he thought. It shouldn't have happened yet.

Holly was so grief-stricken, though, that she couldn't see how upset Joe was. "I know he loved me," she repeated. "If he didn't love me, he wouldn't have gone into the commune after me. Poor Frank."

"He didn't love you!" Joe shouted in exasperation. Holly sat up stiffly and stared at him, pain and doubt in her eyes, and Joe softened. *She's not to blame. There's no reason to yell at her.* "That's just the way he was," he said gently. "He knew you were in trouble and he came to help."

She smiled. "You're a lot like him. Not in the way you walk or dress, of course. He was quieter than you are, and a lot less physical. But both of you believe in the same things, don't you?"

"Yes, I guess we do," Joe said. "Or did. Look, I'd rather not talk about Frank anymore. Not until I have to explain to Mom and Dad."

"So what do you want to talk about?"

"I'd like to sleep," Joe replied, "but if you want to talk, then let's talk about you."

"Me?" Holly said in surprise. "I'm . . . there's nothing to talk about."

*She's hiding something,* Joe realized suddenly. It was in the way her voice trembled, the way she wrapped her arms tightly around herself. "Let's talk about the Rajah, then," he said, playing a hunch.

"What about him?" Holly asked coldly, and he knew he was on the right track. She didn't want to talk about the Rajah.

He had to coax the information out of her. *How would Frank have handled this?* he wondered. He smiled and bent his head so she would not see. When he raised his head again, his expression was bland, as if he weren't really interested in their conversation.

"What made you run to the Rajah?" he asked.

Her relief at his question was noticeable, but there was still a darkness in her eyes and a chill in her voice that bothered Joe. "My father," she said slowly. "I had to get away from my father."

"Why?" Joe asked. "He seems like a nice enough guy to me. Did he hit you?"

"No. He never laid a hand on me. He never even touched me. That was the problem."

"I don't understand."

Holly's eyes flashed angrily. "You've got a family! You hug, don't you? You do things together, like a family should."

"Sure."

"We didn't. My father and I, I mean. Not since Mom died. He didn't love me much before that, but afterward, he *never* had time for me. I didn't even see him at meals.

"It was like he didn't want me there. Like he wanted me to vanish, to be a non-person. There's nothing worse you can do to somebody, Joe. Nothing!

"Nothing," she repeated softly, then she started to cry again. He stood and pulled her to him, hugging her. She clung to him like a child, and after a few minutes, her sobs quieted.

"That explains why you left home," he said gently. "But how did you get hooked up with the cult?"

She pulled away from him, suspicious again. "You're working for my father, aren't you? He's the one who sent you."

"No. He sent our dad. You know him. Fenton Hardy, the detective. He couldn't do anything for you, so we decided to give it a shot."

"So you are working for my father."

Joe shook his head. "He doesn't know what we were doing. Neither does our father. We did it for you, not them. So why don't you trust me?"

"Why should I?" She turned away, arms wrapped around herself. "I trusted Frank. But he's gone now. Why did he have to go?"

"Blame it on the Rajah!" Joe shouted. "He sent his goons after us." Joe calmed himself down. "Look, I'll tell you everything I know. When I was in the Rajah's home, I heard him talking about big plans. You were at the center of them."

Holly gasped. "Me? What do you mean? How could I—?"

"I don't know," Joe replied. "That's why you've got to talk."

She stared at him for a long time. At last she said, "All right.

"It was horrible," she began. "I had to leave home. I couldn't stay there anymore. But I had

92

nowhere to go. My mother had left me some money, so I took it with me. I thought I could live off it for a long time, if I was careful.

"I went to New York. My father probably didn't even notice. By the end of my first day, I had found a cheap hotel to live in. They made you pay by the day, which would make my money run out quicker, but I was going to get a job. There are a lot of acting jobs in New York. I think I'd make a good actress, don't you?

"I would have, too," Holly continued without waiting for Joe to answer. "Every day for a week, I went out and looked for a job. But there were lots of other girls looking, too. I never got to prove myself. It was awful. And I always had this feeling I was being watched, like someone was waiting to get me.

"The first time I noticed any of the Rajah's people, they were dancing outside my hotel. I guess that was three or four days after I got there. They seemed so happy and . . . and loving. And loved. It made me think of everything I wanted and never had. They were a family.

"One day I came back to my room and found I'd been robbed. I'd hidden my money, but it was gone. All of it. So I complained to the manager, and she accused me of trying to get out of paying the rent. She took all my stuff and threw me out. On the street! Where was I supposed to go? All I could do was cry and cry and cry.

"Then he was there.

"He brushed away my tears and called me little sister and told me there was always a place for me among his children. He said that with him, I would be free and safe.

"And I knew I was home.

"I spent the night in the Rajah's center in Manhattan. The next morning, a Rolls-Royce arrived for me. It was the Rajah's, too. He was there to escort me personally to the commune. The others said that marked me as a special follower, and I was. I knew I was.

"For the first time in my life, I felt special and loved. The Rajah treated me like a princess. To this day, I don't know why he did it. But I know I'll always love him."

"Joe?" Holly whispered, but he was asleep. His head bobbed as the train rumbled along, but his eyes didn't open. With her soft, droning voice, she had stopped him when all the Rajah's agents couldn't.

Holly smiled and peered out the door of the boxcar. The train slowed as it neared a railroad yard. They weren't in Bayport, she knew, but they were close enough. It was another of the look-alike, semi-industrial, semirural towns that dotted the banks of the Hudson River. The sweet country smell of the upstate air had been replaced by the odor of sulfur and exhaust.

Holly had hoped she would never see a city again, but there she was.

Joe mumbled, startling her. She watched him carefully to make sure he was still asleep. He murmured something else and rolled onto his side.

Holly studied the empty car, as she had studied it every minute of the long trip. There was nothing in it but Joe and her. She chewed on her lip. There's got to be something here I can use, she thought.

Her eyes lit up, and she moved quickly to one of the doors. It slid shut easily, and much more quietly than she expected. On the door was a metal bar, a support used to keep the door closed. She grabbed the bar and twisted it. It refused to come loose.

Joe rolled onto his stomach.

The train was pulling to a stop. Holly knew the jolt of that final stop would jar Joe awake. She had to work fast.

But the metal bar wouldn't cooperate. Holly braced herself against the door and twisted again. The bar moved slightly. It was old, and the bolts holding it to the door were loose.

She closed her eyes, gritted her teeth, and wedged her hip between the door and the bar. Holding the bar in place with her hands, she threw her weight against the bar. The wood of the door cracked, then splintered.

Joe grumbled at the noise and shook his head, but his eyes stayed closed.

At that moment, the bar broke off in Holly's hands. Catching her breath, she stood over Joe and with both hands raised the bar high over her head. "Goodbye, Joe," she said.

With all her might, she swung the bar down.

# Chapter

## 12

SOMETHING WRAPPED AROUND Holly's ankle and shoved it forward. As she fell back, she tried to scream, but a rough hand clapped over her mouth. The stench of rot filled her nostrils, making her sick. Her arms flapped wildly as she fell, and the iron bar flew from her hand and clattered across the boxcar floor.

Joe shot up. The train lurched to a halt.

Cops, he thought as he saw the two men in the doorway. Train yards hired private guards to keep people off the freight trains. But the men he saw were ragged and unshaven. They looked as if they hadn't slept indoors or eaten in days. Bums, he realized. One of them dragged Holly from the car as the other came inside and picked up the iron bar.

"Money," he said to Joe, and patted the bar

against his palm. The bum spoke in a flat, dull voice. His eyes were dull, too, glazed over by hunger and hate. There was no reason or hope left in him.

Joe didn't move or speak.

"Money!" the bum repeated. He smashed the bar to the floor. Bits of wood flew up from the blow. Joe held his ground.

With a shout, the bum lunged at Joe and swung the iron bar. Joe rolled aside as the bar smashed the floor again. Balancing on his hands, Joe swung his feet around and kicked at the back of the bum's knees. The bum toppled forward.

He caught himself on the iron bar. Without thinking, he flung the bar at Joe, dancing on one foot for a moment, trying to regain his balance. Then his feet spun out from under him, and he flopped like a rag doll onto the floor. A tiny groan sputtered from his lips.

Joe kicked the iron bar out of the car and leaped after it.

Half a car away, Holly wrestled with the other bum, trying to drive him away. It was no use. The bum was much stronger than she was. She dug her fingernails into his cheeks, but the expression in the bum's eyes didn't change. Like the guy in the boxcar, he was beyond pain.

Joe grabbed his shoulder, spun him around, and landed his fist as hard as he could in the bum's belly. The bum doubled over and clutched his stomach. Something woke in his dead eyes, and he growled from his gut.

The bum straightened up as best as he could and threw a punch at Joe. Joe easily sidestepped it and brought both fists down onto the bum's back. The bum sat down suddenly, whining and crying. Joe watched him carefully for a long moment, but the fight had gone out of the bum. He probably doesn't even remember it, Joe realized, and he turned his attention to Holly.

She was kneeling on the ground, shivering with horror. Joe put his hands on her shoulders to help her up, but she wriggled out of his grasp.

"I'm all right," Holly said. "Thanks for helping."

"Those bums won't bother us again," Joe replied. He glanced around the train yard. "There doesn't seem to be anyone else here. Any idea where we are?" She shrugged. "Come on, then," Joe continued, and walked alongside the train.

A head bobbed through the space between two cars. Joe flattened himself against the side of the train, signaling to Holly to do the same. The footsteps on the other side of the train passed by and faded into the distance.

"Let's get out of here," Joe said. He grabbed Holly's hand and pulled her into a run. They sprinted as fast as they could along the row of boxcars.

A whistle pierced the air, and rapid footsteps

began moving toward them. Joe glanced over his shoulder. No one was there, but he could hear more footsteps moving quickly in their direction. They're running alongside the other trains, Joe thought. That's why I can't see them.

He concentrated, sorting out the footsteps. At least six men were after them. From the sound of it, there are four on our left side and two on our right. He might be able to take the two men by himself, but not before the others caught up. There was nowhere to go but forward.

Ahead, he could see the open field beyond the train yard. All they had to do was reach it and climb over the barbed-wire fence surrounding the yard and they were safe. Only a few more steps, he told himself. Just a few more steps.

A bald man with a baseball bat stepped out from behind the caboose and blocked their path.

"We've been waiting for you, boy," he said with a toothless grin. He passed the bat back and forth from hand to hand. "A guy upstate alerted the yard crews all up and down the river that you were on this train, and he's offering a lot of money to get you back."

"Sheriff Keller," Holly gasped. "He's doing this for the Rajah." She slowed to a fast walk. "We can't make it."

"Keep running," Joe ordered. He lowered his head and butted into the man before he could swing the bat. Then he straightened up suddenly, flipping the man over his shoulder.

Holly froze in her tracks. A group of burly men rounded the next train and whooped at her. She whirled around. "Joe!"

"This way!" he shouted, and grabbed her hand again. They dashed back the way they'd come, with the herd of howling men in hot pursuit.

The four men Joe had heard moments earlier spilled through the gaps between the boxcars. Joe veered in the other direction, shoving Holly between two boxcars. The other two men who had been following them would be on the other side, he knew, but he hoped he could handle both of them. If nothing else, he could buy Holly time to escape.

He clenched his fists. Then he hurled himself into the open, hoping to catch the men by surprise. The surprise was on him.

The two men lay on the ground, unconscious.

"What happened to them?" Holly asked in bewilderment.

"Beats me," Joe replied. But he knew. Whoever had knocked out the two men had acted silently and skillfully. And Joe could see no bruises on them, which indicated that their attacker had special talents for dealing with people.

There must be thousands of people like that in the world, he knew, but it was unlikely that any of them would be there at that time and willing to help them.

There's only one person it could be, he thought

to himself. He couldn't suppress a big grin. It was impossible, but it had to be true.

Frank was alive!

"Joe!" Holly screamed again. More men were coming at them. Joe turned. Others were bearing down. It was too late to get away. The men circled them, surrounding them on all sides. Joe counted fourteen all together, coming closer and closer. He could stop three, maybe four at best, but the others would certainly get him.

They were trapped.

Frank, he wondered, where are you when I need you?

He bobbed up and down, looking over the shoulders of the approaching men, but Frank was nowhere to be seen. Apparently, he had his reasons for wanting everyone to think he was dead.

"I'm sorry Holly," Joe said as the men closed in. He clenched and raised his fists. "I let you down."

He slugged the nearest attacker, a bearded man in a denim jacket, and the man toppled like an oak. A fist pounded against Joe's jaw. He staggered back, dazed, and swung without connecting at a second man.

Another fist slammed his shoulder and a third his back. Pain clouded his sight. Joe felt his hand strike something hard, but he couldn't see what it was. He couldn't see anything.

Joe's body had taken over for his mind. He

ignored the pain, swinging wildly as somewhere beyond the cloud around his mind, Holly screamed and screamed until her voice became a long, shrill howl that filled the world.

He was still swinging as the police cars pulled up, sirens blaring. The men scattered at the first sighting of the cars, but Joe kept swinging.

Slowly the cloud lifted from Joe's mind. His arms, terribly tired, fell uselessly to his sides, and he gazed down. Five men lay at his feet. Holly was nearby, jumping up and down, frantically waving at the police.

He realized it was the scream of their sirens, not Holly's screams, that he had heard. He wanted to run again, but he knew that he and Holly could never escape the cars on foot. And maybe I shouldn't, he thought. There's only one person who could have called the police. Frank.

The cars screeched to a halt in front of him, forming a line. As policemen leaped from their cars and took shelter behind them, they took careful aim at Joe. He nodded and sat down on the ground, hands behind his head. A policeman and his partner approached Joe slowly, keeping their guns carefully trained on him. Another policeman led Holly to the cars.

"You're Joe Hardy?" the first policeman asked.

"Yes," Joe replied as the policeman helped him to his feet. "Am I under arrest?"

"Not yet," he replied. "I've got orders to return you to Bayport for questioning. Where's your brother?"

"He was in the caboose the last I saw him," Joe said.

"Check it out, Matt," the policeman said. His partner ran to the caboose and disappeared inside it for a few minutes. Finally he popped his head out a window and yelled, "Nothing in here but some big sacks of grain. No sign of the kid." He came running back.

The first policeman led Joe to the car while his partner opened the back door. Before he got in, Joe took a last look at the train yard. Aside from the police and the few groaning men he had knocked down, there was no movement. Where was Frank?

Okay, big brother, Joe thought as he climbed into the police car. We'll play it your way.

I just hope you know what you're doing.

# Chapter
## 13

THOUGH CHET MORTON had grown up in Bayport, he had never grown tired of the town. With
its clean air and tree-lined streets, it was the only
place he would ever be able to think of as home.
But while Bayport had stayed the same through
much of his childhood, the town had changed a
lot in the past few years, and Chet wasn't sure he
liked all the changes.

Those thoughts were running through his head
as he strolled past the closed-up brick buildings
near the town square. Once they'd been full of
stores. Chet fondly remembered long summer
afternoons in Mr. Reis's Soda Paradise, sipping
strawberry sodas and reading comic books. But
the Soda Paradise was gone, a For Rent sign on
the window of its building.

Other stores were gone, too. They had moved

out to the mall built near the interstate highway that curved around Bayport a few miles out of town. The mall drew the kids, emptying the Soda Paradise until no customers were left.

No customers except Chet, that is. He drank Mr. Reis's sodas right up until the day the shop closed. "You shouldn't drink so many sodas," Mr. Reis would scold. "Are you trying to keep me in business all by yourself?" Chet would laugh then, because he would have kept Mr. Reis in business if he could have.

But the Soda Paradise was gone, and Mr. Reis was gone, too, moved to Miami. Peering into the window of the store, Chet could see that the counter was still there, but it was bare. The comic and magazine racks were empty, and large clumps of dust lay on the floor.

I don't like change, Chet decided. He moved on. The stores were gone, but offices had taken the place of some of them.

But while the new growth would save Bayport from extinction, it would also bring the crime and noise that people were coming to Bayport to get away from. It wasn't something Chet was looking forward to.

Some things would never change, though. The old town square stayed the same, no matter what, with the police station on one side, and City Hall, with the mayor's office and the courthouse in it, on the adjacent side.

Across the square stood the Strand Bank. It

was still the bank most of the people of Bayport used, and it had resisted the move to the mall. But this day, the town square was different. It was lined with rickety old school buses—dozens of them, each carrying forty or more boys and girls. More buses rolled into town every hour, converging on the square, where the marquee on the old movie theater read: TONIGHT ONLY! THE RAJAH SPEAKS!

Chet walked past the town square and turned north on the next block. He didn't want to run into the Rajah's followers congregating there in their turbans and robes.

Though he would never have admitted it, Chet was surprised to see they were actually well behaved. They sat quietly on the buses, chanting their chants. Nothing in their manner indicated that they were any nuisance or threat to the people of Bayport.

Chet pictured himself in a turban and gown, his hair shaved off and a glazed look in his eyes, and he shuddered. He sped up from a fast walk to a jog and didn't slow down until he was far away from the town square.

Chet was almost at the Hardy house when he saw another bus. It was parked across the street from the house. There was no one in the bus, but Chet could see picket signs inside with slogans like THE MURDERER MUST BE PUNISHED and FREE OUR SISTER.

Chet knew the Rajah's people were around

somewhere. He couldn't see them, but he could feel their eyes watching everything that happened on the block. He continued around the block to the next street and approached the Hardy house by the old shortcut through the backyard.

Before he could reach the door, a man appeared in front of Chet, and Chet's heart jumped to his throat. This is it, he thought. They've got me now. I'm doomed. He opened his mouth to scream.

"Kind of jumpy, aren't you, Morton?" Con Riley said, grinning. He was one of the best cops on the Bayport force, but he lived in the shadow of Fenton Hardy and his famous sons. Usually he took this situation with good humor, but he still enjoyed ribbing the Hardys and their friends. "You better get in there, Morton. The chief's waiting for you."

Chet gulped. If Police Chief Collig was there, the meeting would be trouble. For a moment, he considered leaving. But that would mean looking foolish in front of Riley, so Chet opened the screen door and went into the house.

He noticed the change in the house as soon as he entered the kitchen. The room was normally filled with the sweet scent of Aunt Gertrude's baking, and he had hoped to get a slice of cherry pie from her. It was as if she weren't in the house at all. Puzzled, he strolled into the living room.

"It's about time," said Tony Prito, who sat on

the sofa next to Phil Cohen. They were both friends of the Hardys, too. Chet liked Phil, though Phil was·so smart he often made Chet feel stupid by comparison. Tony, who worked at the pizza place in the mall, was okay, but Chet thought he was a show-off and didn't quite trust him.

"We're about to get our orders," Phil said with a smile. There was something reassuring about Phil. No matter how great the danger, he never lost his sense of humor, and Chet had the feeling they were heading for danger now. "Allow the chief to explain."

Chief Collig stood next to the easy chair. He was clearly uncomfortable. Though he had often asked Fenton Hardy for help, he never liked putting the boys in danger.

"In case there are any of you who don't know," he began, "a couple of days ago, Frank and Joe Hardy rescued Holly Strand from this madman who calls himself the Rajah. Today the Rajah has brought his people to town in an attempt to get the girl back. And Frank Hardy is still missing."

Chet heard footsteps on the stairs and looked up to see Joe Hardy. "Hello, Joe," he said uncomfortably.

Joe had been involved with Chet's sister, Iola, until she was killed by a bomb meant for Joe. It was the event that had given Joe and Frank a new direction in their lives, as dedicated crime fighters. But it had left Joe and Chet unsure of what to say to each other.

"Hi," Joe replied. Then he said to the chief, "I don't think it's as simple as that."

"Wait a minute!" Chet cried. "I thought you were in jail. Didn't the police bring you in yesterday?"

The chief shook his head. "There's not enough evidence to hold him. The Rajah has turned over a gun with Joe's fingerprints on it, but he won't let anyone see the body of the man who was supposedly killed. He's a strange one."

"And all the witnesses are his followers, which makes it a little hard for the police to trust them," Joe added. "But it does restrict my movements."

"Yes," Chief Collig agreed. "Until we've sorted it out, you're still a suspect. I'm afraid you'll have to stay in the house."

Joe nodded. "Which is why we need you and Tony and Phil, Chet. You're going to be my eyes and legs. As I was saying, the Rajah's up to something that's bigger than just getting Holly back.

"She told me how his people followed her when she ran away from home. He finally came looking for her *personally* and took her up to his commune *himself*. No one else got that kind of special treatment.

"Then, when I was in the Rajah's home, I heard him arguing with his assistant, Vivasvat.

Vivasvat called himself Shakey Leland and called the Rajah Mikey."

"Leland, huh?" the chief said. "I remember him. He used to run con games up in the Boston area. I ran him out of Bayport a couple of times, but he vanished a few years back. No wonder the Rajah doesn't want us looking at the body."

"There's more," Joe said. "He knew who Frank was before Frank got into the commune. He knew who I was. So he must have *let* us take Holly out of there."

"That doesn't make sense," Tony mused. "If he went to all that much trouble, why would he let her go? And then come after her?"

"It puzzled me, too," said a voice behind them. "There's only one explanation I can think of." They all spun abruptly and stared at the tall, brown-haired boy who leaned against the kitchen doorway.

"Holly's more valuable to the Rajah here," said Frank Hardy.

# Chapter

## 14

"FRANK!" JOE CRIED. "You're back! I *thought* you were alive, but when you didn't show yourself . . . What have you been *doing?*"

"A little nosing around—while the Rajah and his people thought I was dead," Frank said. "I took advantage of the dark and chucked a grain sack off the caboose. That's what fell into the river."

"Great trick!" Phil Cohen said. "But how'd you manage to sneak back here without the Rajah's people spotting you?"

"I know my way around Bayport a lot better than the cultists do," Frank said with a smile. "Like the old shortcuts we used when we were kids." He looked around. "But where are Mom and Dad?"

"Fenton's guarding Emmett Strand and his

daughter. I've called to tell him you're all right,'' Chief Collig said. "He sent your mother and your aunt out of town until all this blows over. They'll be glad to know you're back.''

"What did you mean, Frank?'' Chet asked. "You said something about the Rajah needing Holly out here?''

Frank pursed his lips, thinking. "She holds some special meaning for him. What's special about Holly? She's pretty enough and smart, but what's extraordinary about her?''

"Her father?'' Phil suggested.

"The bank!'' Tony shouted.

"Exactly,'' Frank said. "The Rajah plans to rob the Strand Bank.''

"I don't get it,'' Joe said. "How can Holly help him rob the bank? Even if she could get him in there, computers control the vault doors. No one can get to the money without the proper control codes. It would've made more sense for the Rajah to hold Holly hostage in exchange for the codes.''

The chief cleared his throat. "It doesn't matter. Now that we've figured out his scheme, we'll just arrest the Rajah the instant he sets foot inside Bayport. That will take care of him.''

"But not his followers,'' Frank said. "We haven't got any proof of the Rajah's plans, and you can't arrest him without proof. If you do, there'll be a riot. Can you imagine five thousand teenagers on a rampage in Bayport?''

"Five thousand!" Chief Collig gasped. "Surely there aren't that many?"

"There are," Frank said. "Every follower he has in the world. They're all in Bayport.

"And so is he."

Fenton Hardy pulled aside the curtain and looked out the front window of Emmett Strand's house. He was annoyed that none of the Rajah's followers were visible outside. They were out there somewhere, probably watching him even as he was looking for them, and he would have felt better if he could see them.

Instincts developed over long years of detective work told him that the enemy was nearby. And he had learned to trust his instincts.

Maybe, he thought, they didn't know where Strand lived. Unlike most other people with money, Emmett Strand lived in a small house. Since his wife died, Strand had shown little interest in anything but banking, and moving would have taken a lot of time and attention. So he stayed in his modest home with, until recently, his daughter.

"Would you like some tea, Mr. Hardy?" Holly called from the next room.

"Yes, please," he called back. He would have preferred coffee, but he saw no reason to thwart Holly's good intentions. He had seen Emmett Strand do that too often in the past few years, on those rare occasions when he had visited Emmett in his home.

Emmett Strand was always contradicting Holly, always making her feel as if nothing she could do were good enough. There was no malice in what he did, just awkwardness. He had left Holly's upbringing to his wife. Turned into a single parent, he had no idea of what to do, and he was too proud a man to ask.

Was it any wonder that Holly Strand had run away from home?

Fenton Hardy wondered at the change in Holly since her return to Bayport. Surly and short-tempered before leaving, she had become sweet and contrite, anxious to help. He shook his head. People, in his experience, did not change their natures so quickly.

Holly entered the room, carrying a tea tray with a silver teapot and a china cup on it. Next to the cup was a little silver spoon, a sugar bowl, and several slices of lemon. Fenton poured himself a cup of tea and squeezed a lemon into it.

"Can I talk to you?" Holly asked. "About Frank?"

Fenton Hardy looked at her over the rim of his cup as he sipped. No one was supposed to know that Frank was alive. "Go ahead," he said.

Holly bowed her head and giggled in embarrassment. "I'm sorry. I know you think something has happened to Frank, but . . . somehow I feel he's okay. I can . . . I don't know . . . I just know he's out there.

"What I wanted to know is—" She took a deep breath, steeling herself. "Is he serious about Callie?"

"Callie Shaw?" Fenton Hardy chuckled. "I don't really know. He sees her pretty exclusively." He gulped down more tea to hide his amusement.

The smile faded from Holly's lips, and she cast her eyes to the floor. "Oh. I guess there's no room for me in his life, then."

"I wouldn't give up too quickly," Fenton replied, stifling a chuckle. "Frank has always been a little shy around girls. I've always suspected he stayed with Callie because she was safe. Now, you take Joe. *He's* a real ladies' man. . . ."

His head spun suddenly. The room seemed to wave past him. "Now, you take Joe . . ." he said again, but the words turned to gum in his mouth. His fingers grew numb, and the cup slid from them. It fell to the floor but bounced instead of breaking, and warm liquid ran from it onto the rug.

The rug rose up and slammed him in the face. He rolled onto his back. "Help me," he tried to say, but his mouth wouldn't move properly. Holly stood over him, studying him. Her warm smile had vanished, replaced by a cold glower.

Then darkness swam over him, and he remembered nothing else.

Holly squatted and picked up the fallen teacup. As the Rajah had instructed, she wiped the cup clean of knockout drops.

She walked up the stairs to her father's study. He was sleeping at his desk, where she had left him. She picked his teacup off the floor and wiped it clean, too.

"Can you hear me, Daddy?" she asked.

With eyes closed, he nodded his head slightly. His lips twitched as if he were trying to talk, but no words came out.

"Tell me the control codes to the vault, Daddy," she said.

Emmett Strand mumbled and rolled his head onto his shoulder.

"Daddy!" she snapped. "This is important." She lifted his hand and put a pen in it, then rested it on a piece of paper on the desk. "Write it down, Daddy."

Without waking, he began to write.

The desk phone rang. Holly snatched it from its cradle, worried that the noise would wake her father. To her relief, he continued writing. At the sound of the voice on the other end of the line, she snapped to attention. "Yes, I gave him the truth serum, just as you said. He's writing now." Her father's hand slid off the table.

She picked up the paper and read it over the phone.

"What do you mean, the Rajah's in Bayport?" the chief asked Frank. "We've been watching the roads since the first bus rolled in."

"When I left Joe and Holly at the train yard, I began walking back to Bayport," Frank said. "It was a long walk, but I didn't have any other choice. If I had hitched a ride or hopped another train, I would have been caught. So I walked.

"I was just getting to the Bayport town limits when I was nearly spotted by a passing car. There was a ditch by the side of the road and I jumped into it. Imagine my surprise when I recognized the people in the car."

"The Rajah?" Chet asked.

Frank laughed. "Good guess, Einstein. That was a few hours before his followers came rolling into town."

"Impossible!" Chief Collig muttered. "Joe described the Rajah's Rolls-Royce perfectly. There's no way it could have gotten in without getting spotted."

"That's just it," Frank said. "He didn't use the Rolls-Royce. He came here in an old, beat-up Volkswagen. You have to hand it to the Rajah. He knows how to keep a low profile when he wants one.

"Anyway, once I got to town, it wasn't too hard to find the car. The Rajah's holed up in the old Miller Hotel on the square, under the name of Michael Hadley."

"Mikey!" Joe said. "That's what Shakey Leland called him."

"And he's in the square," the chief said in horror. "He could touch off that crowd in an instant. I'll send Riley over to arrest him before he can cause any more trouble."

"You can't charge him with anything," Frank reminded him. "But maybe we can head him off before he carries out his plans.

"Phil, use my computer and call some law enforcement data bases. Try to find something on a Michael Hadley who hung around with a Shakey Leland.

"Chet, I want you to keep an eye on the Miller Hotel. We've got to know when the Rajah makes his move.

"Tony, find Biff Hooper. We'll need all the friends we have—especially ones with muscle. As soon as you find him, head over to the Strand place and help protect Holly. When everything breaks loose, she'll be in danger."

The back door slammed, and Con Riley burst into the room. The color was drained from his face, and for the first time since Frank and Joe had met him, he looked like he was verging on panic.

"The call came in on the radio, Chief," Riley said. "We've got to get over to the square.

"It's a riot."

# Chapter

## 15

THE SQUARE WAS on fire.

Mad shadows of a thousand-headed monster rose up on the wall of City Hall, cast there by the flames. They roared across the grassy park in the midst of the square.

They haven't spread to the buildings yet, Frank realized. It can be stopped. From somewhere he heard sirens but couldn't tell if they were from police cars or fire engines. They must be fire engines, he thought. All the cops are here already.

Policemen in black, faceless helmets dashed back and forth in the streets, chasing the Rajah's followers. As they ran, the Rajah's people picked up rocks and hurled them at the pursuing police. Waving nightsticks, the policemen forced back the rioters as best they could, trying to stem the flood of violence.

"It's no good," Chief Collig said suddenly to Frank. "We haven't got enough men to handle a riot this big. The mayor will have to call in the National Guard."

Bayport will be in ruins long before they get here, thought Frank. He turned to speak to the chief, but Collig was already gone to help his men.

Across the square, glass smashed. Frank looked over to see the front window of the police station falling away, shattered by a rock.

Nearby, Joe pulled three rioters off a policeman who had fallen. Panicked, the policeman swung at Joe with his nightstick. Joe hopped out of the way and was swallowed up by the crowd.

A mist hit Frank, startling him. Firemen had arrived, spraying the grass fire with a jet of water that turned the flame into thick black smoke. The smoke billowed over the square, darkening the late afternoon.

Frantic policemen whispered to the firemen, who turned the hose on some rioters and drove them back and out of the square.

Frank heard more windows breaking, somewhere to the south. The riot was moving out of the square and into the residential areas of Bayport, he knew. No one seemed to notice him. He was looking for a familiar face, one that could bring the riot to an end.

He was looking for the Rajah.

Instead, he found Joe. In an alley, Joe had

cornered one of the Rajah's guards, a brown-bearded man with beady eyes and bad teeth. He growled at Joe through a twisted mouth, and his hand crept slowly around his back.

"Trouble, brother?" Frank yelled over the din of the crowd.

"I know this guy," Joe replied. "The last time I saw him, I had to take a Magnum away from him. His name's Bobby. He was just going to tell me what the Rajah's real scheme is."

Bobby's hand swung behind his back and came out again with a Walther automatic pistol.

The alley exploded in a cloud of gas. Joe choked and leaped forward, slamming into Bobby. He slugged the Rajah's guard with all his strength. Bobby crumpled to the ground, the Walther sliding from his hand as he slid down the wall. Joe kicked the gun into a pile of rubbish.

Then he coughed and doubled over. Fire burned his eyes and nose, but there was no fire. He rubbed his face, trying to put it out. The more he rubbed, the hotter the fire grew. His stomach began to churn. He felt like passing out. He wanted to stop coughing, but he couldn't.

Frank caught Joe's arm and helped him out of the alley. The elder Hardy brother was coughing too, and crying, but while Joe had fought Bobby, Frank had stripped off his jacket and tied it around his nose and mouth. "We got hit with tear gas," he told Joe. "Relax. Don't rub or it gets worse. Just let the wind blow it out of your eyes, and you'll be okay."

Only half-able to see, they stumbled through the streets, staggering into rioters who barely noticed them. The Rajah's thousand-headed monster had broken up into five thousand frightened teenagers, all running in different directions, pursued by the law.

Frank knew what the terror in their faces meant. It meant that the Rajah's hold over them was broken at last. He had abandoned them to the police, and that breach of faith could never be repaired.

A team of policemen in gas masks and riot gear stopped, recognized the Hardy boys, and moved on. Slowly moisture returned to Joe's throat, and the coughing subsided. He was able to see again. Another squad of policemen raced through the clearing smoke, and then two boys appeared— Tony Prito and Biff Hooper.

"Are you guys all right?" Tony asked. "We came over as soon as I rounded up Biff. What happened? It looks like a war zone out here."

It was true. Much of the park was burned away, and the smell of smoke clung to everything. Broken glass littered the sidewalks. The scene was like something out of a war movie.

"It doesn't make sense," Frank said. "Why would the Rajah throw away his cult like that? He practically sacrificed them!"

"And half of Bayport with them," Joe murmured. "What's his game?"

Biff twirled a finger around his ear. "Aw, you know his kind of creep. Crazy."

Frank and Joe scowled, but Tony laughed. "Yeah, every cop in town is out chasing his followers. He didn't even have the guts to be here with his people."

Frank gasped. *"Every* cop? You sure of that?"

"Positive," Tony replied. "Chief Collig superseded all other orders when the riot started—"

He never got a chance to finish. "The bank!" Frank and Joe shouted at the same time. In a second, both were on their feet, racing for the Strand Bank.

When they reached it, they saw five men inside, dressed in black leather jackets. They held Uzi submachine guns in their hands. One of them was on his knees in front of Emmett Strand's desk, tapping on a computer punchboard hidden under the desk drawer.

Peering through the window, Joe recognized one of the men. It was the other man who had held him up on the road outside the commune. "Those are the Rajah's men," he whispered to Frank. "But where's the Rajah? What are they doing?"

"Opening the vault," Frank whispered back. Tony and Biff caught up with them and hid themselves along the granite wall of the bank. "I don't know how, but they've got the computer access code."

"Not from old Strand," Joe said. He frowned. He knew Emmett Strand shared the information with no one at the bank. Someone else had provided the information, someone who had enough contact with Strand to be able to get it out of him. "Holly," he gasped.

"What?" Frank whispered.

"It all fits," Joe said. *"That's* why the Rajah had us take Holly out of the commune. So she could go home 'saved' and wheedle the access codes from her father."

"You're talking crazy," Frank shot back. But he had a sinking feeling that Joe was right. They had been used, and because of it, the Rajah's agents were about to reap millions of dollars.

Except that the Hardys hadn't died when they were supposed to. And that would be the Rajah's downfall, if Frank had anything to say about it.

"Frank!" Phil Cohen shouted from across the square. He ran toward them, waving a computer printout. "You've got to see this!"

Frank tried to signal him to hide himself, but it was too late. The square, abandoned by rioters and police, was silent as the grave by now, and Phil's words echoed through it like thunderclaps. The gunman nearest the door burst out, aiming at Phil.

Biff tackled the gunman. The Uzi flew from his

hands and skidded along the sidewalk. Joe lunged for it.

A burst of gunfire ripped between him and the gun. A second gunman stood there, aiming at them. Across the street, Phil froze. The second gunman signaled him over. One by one, the boys got up and raised their hands over their heads.

"What'd you shoot for?" the first gunman said to his partner as he got to his feet. He picked up the fallen gun. "If any cops heard that—"

"If the brats have done their job properly, they'll be leading the cops out of town by now," the second gunman replied. "Let's get these punks inside. These two"—he pointed at the Hardys—"deserve to watch us rob this place. After all, we couldn't have done it without them."

The gunmen's laughter roared mockingly in the Hardys' ears as they were led inside.

"Where's the Rajah?" Joe asked. "I can't believe he trusts you not to run off with the money yourselves."

"Shut up," the first gunman snarled. "This money is ours. He doesn't want any of it."

"Sort of a reward for his faithful servants?" Frank quipped. But he was stumped. If money wasn't the Rajah's game, what was?

The gunmen ignored him. "That's the last sequence," said the one on the floor. He stood up as the bank vault clicked and whirred. Slowly the vault door swung open.

"This is it! We're rich!" a gunman cried, but surprise choked his words. Stunned and bewildered, everyone stared at one another, then at the vault, and then at one another again.

The vault was empty.

"So, the Rajah cheated you, too," Frank said calmly.

# Chapter

## 16

"THAT MAN IS a smooth operator, all right," Frank went on. "He's got the money, and he left you here to get grabbed by the cops."

"Shut up!" shouted the gunman nearest the vault. "You're nothing but trouble, punk. I ought to ice you right here."

"You just can't stand the truth," Frank said, raising his voice. The other gunmen turned to watch the fight. I've got to keep them looking at me, Frank thought, and continued, "You're so dumb you think you'd still be tough even if you didn't have that Uzi."

The gunman sneered. "Keep talking, kid. Think I was born yesterday? I'm not putting down the gun no matter what you say."

While everyone's attention was on Frank, Joe slowly sidled up to the gunman nearest him.

"You're chicken," Frank said. "You're too chicken to even find the Rajah and get your money."

The gunman steadied the submachine gun at Frank. "I ought to shut you up right now."

"Hold it, Duke," another gunman said. "The kid's got a point. What are we going to do about the Rajah?"

"Shut up!" the one called Duke screamed.

Joe leaped for the gunman nearest him.

At the sound of a safety clicking off, Joe and the other boys threw themselves to the floor. Duke spun, pivoting away from Frank and riddling the wall of the bank with bullets. One of the gunmen shrieked and fell back, clutching his shoulder. Duke had gotten one of his own men.

But he had turned his back on Frank. Striking a karate pose, Frank lunged forward, smashing the heel of his hand against Duke's back. His face frozen with anger, Duke spun as he fell, trying to get a shot at Frank again. Frank clutched the gun stock and kicked Duke away. The gunman slammed against the bank's marble wall and sank, groaning, to the floor.

Frank turned and aimed the Uzi at the other gunmen. "We can do this the hard way," he said. "But if anyone starts shooting, I guarantee at least one of you won't get out of here."

The gunmen glanced from one to the other, silently weighing their options. "You going after the Rajah?'' one of them asked. ''You going to catch him?''

Frank nodded. ''You know I am. We will, my brother and I.''

The gunmen exchanged glances again. Slowly the one who had spoken crouched and set his gun on the floor. Then he stood again, his hands raised high in the air. ''If it's all right with you, I want to live long enough to pay that creep back,'' he said.

One by one, the other gunmen set their weapons down and surrendered. The boys got up from the floor and gathered the guns.

''I don't get it,'' Tony said. ''How did this Rajah rob the bank? There wasn't time after the riot started. He *couldn't* have gotten here before his men.''

''He had plenty of time,'' Frank said. ''The riot wasn't his cover, the incoming buses were. We were paying so much attention to his followers that we missed what he was up to. If he had the access codes, he could have come in here any time. The riot was just icing on the cake.''

''So he only wanted the money, after all,'' Joe said. ''I thought it was something more than that.''

''So did I,'' Frank said. ''I still do. There's something here that just doesn't add up.''

''That's what I've been trying to tell you,'' Phil Cohen said. ''I did the computer check, like you told me to. There's no criminal record on Michael Hadley. So I checked on Shakey Leland.

"It seems our Mr. Leland took over a carnival late in his criminal career. It took a little work to get the carnival's tax records, but when I did, who do you think I found listed as a mind reader and fortune-teller?"

"Michael Hadley," Tony said in a bored tone. He hated it when Phil belabored the obvious.

Phil grinned and shook his head. "Not quite." He offered the computer readout to Frank. "I figured you'd want to see this."

Joe moved beside his brother for a look at the paper, and their faces turned gray as they read it.

Frank tossed the Uzi to Biff. "Can you hold these clowns until the police get back?"

"Just let them try to start something with me," Biff replied. He gritted his teeth, showing them to the gunmen.

"Good," Frank said. "Get some medical attention for the one who got shot, too. We'll be back as soon as we can." With Tony and Phil in tow, the Hardy boys started for the door.

"Wait a minute!" Biff yelled. "What's up? Where are you going?"

"We've got to get to the Strand house right away," Frank said without stopping.

"As for what's up," Joe said, "you'd never believe it."

*     *     *

Fenton Hardy tried to lift his head. It wouldn't move. He wanted to use his hands to raise it, but they wouldn't move, either. They hung at his sides, pressing against cool metal.

He tried to remember where he was. Slowly the dull fog lifted from his brain. He was in a house, and he was gagged and bound to a chair. Emmett's house, he remembered. What had happened? He recalled watching for the Rajah's followers, and then Holly brought him some tea, and then nothing.

The tea! he realized. She drugged the tea.

"Wake up," he heard a deep voice say. "Wake up, Fenton Hardy. We need a witness." A hand lifted his head by the hair, and he found himself staring at a muscular, dark-eyed man, dressed in silk. He towered over Hardy like a giant. Still dazed from the drug, Hardy shifted his eyes. Emmett Strand was tied to the chair next to him, and Emmett's sad eyes were focused on something beyond the tall man.

Then the man let go of Hardy's hair and stepped aside, and Fenton Hardy saw what Emmett Strand saw.

There, dressed in fine purple silks, was Holly Strand. She stood contentedly, a vacant gleam in her eyes, which were fixed on the tall man. In her hand was a butcher knife.

"We need a witness," the tall man repeated, "to the trial and execution of Emmett Strand."

Fenton Hardy strained at the ropes that bound

him to the chair, but they held firm. He knew, finally, whom he faced. It was the Rajah. Hardy had never seen the man before, but he understood the mad gleam in his eye. Before, Fenton Hardy believed the Rajah was nothing more than a clever con man, out to swindle children of their property and their futures. But face-to-face with the Rajah, he knew how wrong he had been.

For the Rajah had the look of a man who listened to voices in his head, who firmly believed in his own superiority. It was a look Fenton Hardy had seen in many other men, men who viewed the world through their own fantasies of power.

"This man has committed many crimes," the Rajah said, resting a bony hand on Strand's shoulder. "He takes money from the poor and keeps it for himself."

"It's not true," Strand mumbled, his voice cracking.

"He has cared for no one. He has treated his business as more important than love, friends, or family. He has condemned his children to smother in the emptiness of their own souls."

"No," Strand said, a little louder now. "I've only got one child. Holly. I've always loved her. I always wanted the best for her."

"Old man," the Rajah spat. "You lie!"

He stepped away from Strand, circling around Holly. She didn't take her eyes off him. Her faith in him, Fenton Hardy could see, was total and absolute. She would work for the Rajah, she would die for him if necessary.

She would even kill for him.

"Your life has been dedicated to taking, old man," the Rajah continued. He wrapped a comforting arm around Holly. "You have robbed your precious daughter of her childhood. You robbed your wife of life itself. For these things, you stand convicted."

"No," Strand murmured. "Please . . . don't . . ."

"As you have taken from others," the Rajah said, "so have I taken from you. I have taken everything. I have taken the money from your bank, and by doing this, I have taken your reputation. I have taken your daughter from you and given her a home where she is loved as a little sister. I have taken your peace of mind.

"As you took everything from me, I take everything from you."

Emmett Strand stared at the Rajah, stunned. "From you? I've never even met you before! How could I take anything from you?"

"Silence!" The Rajah's eyes flared as if on fire, and his smug sneer vanished, replaced by lips curled in rage. "You are a hypocrite."

Holly stepped over to her father and raised the knife over his head.

"And now we take your life," the Rajah said.

# Chapter

# 17

"WHAT GIVES?" ASKED Tony as they ran. "The Rajah's got what he came for. He'll be long gone by now."

"No," Joe said. "Frank was right all along. The Rajah isn't out for money alone. He wants revenge."

They turned a corner and broke into a sprint. At the far end of the block was the Strand house. Dusk had fallen, and the house was dark, except for a single light on the second floor.

"I don't like it," said Frank. "There's no sign of Dad, but he wouldn't leave. Not unless something has happened." Or something has happened to him, he thought, and forced the thought from his mind.

"Would someone *please* tell me what's going on?" Tony demanded.

"It's really very simple," Phil replied. "See, the Rajah used to work in the carnival with Shakey Leland, where he learned tricks like mind reading and hypnotism."

Tony was puzzled. "I thought you said Michael Hadley isn't the Rajah!"

Phil laughed. "Not quite. I said the Rajah isn't Michael Hadley. Not really, anyway."

"Shhh," Frank said. He bounded up the front steps and onto the porch of the Strand place. He tried the front door. It was locked.

"Dad!" he called. "Holly!" There was no answer. "Something's wrong. We've got to break the door down."

"Let me," Joe said. He hurled himself against the heavy oak door. It held. "I'll try it again."

"Never mind," Frank said, and peeled off his jacket. He wrapped it around his fist and rammed his hand through the front window. The glass broke and spilled into the house. A loud bell sounded, part of the house's burglar alarm system, and somewhere in the Bayport police station, a light on a map of the town started to blink—a light that was unwatched, since the entire force was trying desperately to round up the rioting cultists.

With his wrapped hand, Frank knocked the rest of the glass out of the window. Peeling his jacket away, he reached a hand inside the house and unlatched the window.

In seconds, they climbed inside. "There was a

light on upstairs," Frank said. "We'll try there."

Praying that they were not too late, Frank bolted up the stairs.

"Kill him, little sister," the Rajah said. "Make him feel the pain that you have felt."

Holly stood with the butcher knife poised over her father. "Yes," she said gently, as if in a trance. She forced the blade down.

Outside the room an alarm bell clanged.

The sound startled her, and she pulled the knife away before it struck her father. She stared at the blade in her hands, holding it as if it were a snake that would coil around and strike her.

"Little sister," the Rajah snarled. "Do as you are told."

"No, please," Emmett Strand pleaded. "I know I haven't shown it very often, Holly, but—" He paused, unsure of how to say what he had to say. He could think of only one way. "Baby, I love you."

The door crashed in, and Frank Hardy stood there, glaring at the knife in Holly's hand. Looking at the cruel leer on the Rajah's face, he understood what was happening.

"Don't do it," he said to Holly. "Stop right now. For me."

Slowly she shook her head. "He doesn't love me."

"Of course he loves you," Frank said. "He's your father."

"Do you love me, Frank?" she asked. "I want you to love me."

"And I do," he replied. "But not in the way you want."

"That's what I'd expect *him* to say!" Holly cried bitterly, looking down at her father.

"He deserves to die," the Rajah said. "Kill him."

She held the knife uncertainly, waving it over her father's head.

"Listen to me, Holly," Frank said. "I know what you're going through. We all want to be loved."

"You do not know!" she screamed. "Everyone loves you! Your mother and father love you! Your brother loves you! Callie Shaw loves you! I love you!"

He shook his head. "And everyone loves you, Holly. Your father loves you. I love you. But people love in different ways. You can't choose the way people are going to love you. You have to take what you get. That's just the way it is."

"I'm the only one who loves you, little sister," the Rajah said. "Do as I say."

"No!" Frank shouted. "He doesn't love anyone! He hates, Holly! He hates! Do you want to be like that? Do you want to be like him?"

"She *is* like me," the Rajah said smugly. "She is my little sister."

Frank turned and looked him in the eye. In a calm voice, he said, "I know." Then he smiled.

For the first time, doubt crept into the Rajah's eyes. "You don't know what you're talking about."

"I do," Frank said. "I had a check done on your background, Paul."

"You've mistaken me for someone else," the Rajah said with trembling lips. "I am the Rajah, he through whom heaven shall be made on earth. I am the mightiest of mighties, and nations shall tremble before me."

"You were a cheap hustler in a carnival," Frank interrupted. He was suddenly very tired and short-tempered. "Your name was Mikey Hadley when Shakey Leland found you pitching fortunes for a couple of dollars a shot.

"He must have been pretty impressed with your talent. Then again, I hear you were a fair hypnotist, and Leland was smart enough to know the time was ripe for a new religion."

"No," said the Rajah.

"Yes," Frank continued. "So you and Leland bought a little land and started preaching, preying on poor, lost kids who had run away from home. You promised them heaven, but you just made them your brainwashed slaves."

"It was my divine right," the Rajah said.

"But you never told Leland what you were really up to, did you? You kept your eyes open for Holly, because you knew someday she'd walk into your trap, or you would lure her in or drag her in, and then you could carry out your plans.

"But Leland was smart enough to see that your revenge scheme would blow the good scam you two had. So you killed him to keep him from getting in the way. Right?"

"Silence!" the Rajah raged. His hands shook as he squeezed them into fists.

Emmett Strand stared dumbly at Frank. "What are you talking about?" he asked, but a look of terrible understanding began to steal over his face. The past was coming back to Strand, and it terrified him.

Frank stared into Holly's eyes. What he was saying fascinated her, but he could see that she was frightened, too, and in that state she was capable of anything.

He reached over and took the knife from her hand. She didn't try to hold on to it.

"The Rajah never told you his real name, did he?" Frank asked her. "Not the name he was using when Leland found him. His real name."

"Stop!" the Rajah shouted. "I command it!"

Frank ignored him. "I saw his birth certificate, Holly. Michael's his second name. Hadley is his mother's last name.

"His name is Paul Michael Strand."

"Mary Hadley had a son?" Emmett Strand said in disbelief. Tears welled up in his eyes. "I never knew. . . . I never knew. . . ."

"You knew!" the Rajah shrieked. Despite his size, he no longer seemed the nearly omnipotent figure he had appeared to be just moments before.

He looked like an angry little boy, and years of rage crackled in his voice.

"My mother wasn't good enough for you! You had to go off and run your bank and make lots of money, and you didn't care about us or anyone else. All you cared about was your money."

"It's not true," Strand said. "I didn't know. Do you mean all these years you thought that I—? Oh, you poor boy. My poor son."

"I don't want your pity, old man!" the Rajah said. "I don't need it."

"You've got nothing else, Paul," Frank said. "Your followers have left you. You're wanted by the police. Give it up."

To Frank's surprise, the Rajah smiled. "You think you have power over me because you've discovered my secret? The voices still speak to me." He tapped two fingers on his forehead. "They have told me my future, and it is good."

He stretched out his hand to Holly. "Come with me, little sister."

She looked to Frank, but though she moved her lips, no words came out. She was confused, Frank realized. She was in shock, and he wasn't sure what to do.

Before anyone could move, Holly stepped over to the Rajah and took his hand.

"No!" Frank screamed, but it was too late.

The Rajah spun her as soon as her fingers touched his. As she twirled into him, his arm wrapped around her neck and shoulders, holding her there. A hand disappeared into his silk robe and came out a second later, holding a gun. He pressed the barrel of the gun against Holly's temple.

"Now," the Rajah said, "I will have my revenge."

# Chapter

# 18

"LET HER GO!" Frank shouted at the Rajah. "It's all over. You've lost."

The Rajah's mouth twitched in anger. Then his lips curled into a vicious smile. Madness glazed his eyes.

"My father has sinned, and he must pay," the Rajah said. "Vengeance is mine, sayeth the Lord. From this day, I am the Lord, and I shall avenge."

Firmly holding Holly, he turned the gun on Frank. "You thought you could trick me, but I know. Call in the others."

"What others?" Frank asked.

"You came with three others. Your brother and two boys. Call them in, or this precious flower will be crushed." The Rajah tightened his grip on Holly.

He does know! Frank thought. For a moment, he was in the Rajah's grip again, as he had almost been at the commune. He was ready to believe that the Rajah had miraculous powers. He shook himself, pulling his eyes away from the Rajah's magnetic gaze. There's a simple explanation for this. He saw us from the window, that's all.

"Three seconds," the Rajah said.

"Joe!" Frank called. "Tony! Phil! Come in here."

One by one, they entered. The Rajah gestured with the pistol, and they raised their hands and moved next to Frank. "Very good," the Rajah said. "Turn around and put your hands and faces against the wall." They followed his orders.

"Very good," he repeated. Still gripping Holly, he turned to Emmett Strand. "I bless you, Father." He aimed the gun at Strand.

His fingered tightened on the trigger.

Fenton Hardy threw himself forward into the Rajah. He was still tied in his chair, and he swung his body as he lunged so that the heavy chair smashed into the Rajah's side.

The shot slammed into the side wall.

"Hiiii-ya!" Frank screamed at the top of his lungs as he spun and leaped into the air. He jabbed his heel out, smacking it against the Rajah's gun hand. The gun flew across the room. Frank landed and swung the back of his hand into the side of the Rajah's head.

With a scream, the Rajah let go of Holly and

144

raised a hand to his pained ear. Before anyone could stop her, Holly scrambled across the room and grabbed the gun.

Her face was lit with anger and hate as she aimed it at the Rajah. "You used me," she said bitterly. "I thought you were good. I thought you loved me for myself."

Hunched over in pain, the Rajah stared at her in disbelief. "Little sister," he said, but the strength was gone from his voice. He had offered peace to his followers, but now, staring at death, he was terrified. Almost by reflex, he continued, "Don't turn on me. You were chosen above all others—"

"Shut up!" she shouted. Tears of rage blinded her.

"Give me the gun, Holly," Frank said. He stepped forward, his hand extended. "If you shoot him, you'll be as bad as he is. Don't let his lies destroy your life."

"I am destroyed!" she howled. "I've been such a fool!" She held the gun steady in both hands and drew a bead on the Rajah's heart. Her finger twitched on the trigger.

Then, with a tiny cry of frustrated anger, she thrust the gun into Frank's hands and sank to her knees, sobbing.

In a superhuman burst of desperation, the Rajah hurled himself at Joe and the other boys. Instinctively they jumped out of the way.

Laughing madly, the Rajah plunged through

the window, spraying glass across the sloping roof outside. He rolled down the roof and crashed clumsily onto the ground. When he stood, he was still laughing.

"Call Chief Collig," Frank ordered. He helped his father off the floor. "The police can pick up the Rajah now."

"The police are too busy to help," Joe said. "I'm going after him." Before anyone could speak, Joe leaped out the window and slid down the roof in pursuit.

By the time he reached the ground, the Rajah was already rounding the far corner of the block. Joe sprinted after him. For Joe, it was just like running in one of his high school track meets. Except this is more important than any race, he thought. If I don't stop the Rajah now, he'll keep coming back until he wins. He'll wipe us out one by one when we least expect it.

Just like what happened to Iola. He swallowed the lump in his throat. He was going to catch the Rajah if it was the last thing he did.

But the Rajah was faster than Joe expected. Already he was out of sight, leaving only a trail of mirthless, mocking laughter for Joe to follow.

He turned onto the next street as the laughter turned to howling. There he saw the Rajah, haranguing someone he had knocked on the ground. When he saw Joe, he began to run again, but he had lost precious time, and Joe was close on his heels.

Gasping for breath, Joe poured all his energy into a last burst of speed and tackled the Rajah.

"Release me," the Rajah ordered. "I am the power—"

"Shut up," Joe barked, and twisted the Rajah's arm behind his back, immobilizing him. "This time it's really over."

"Joe!" called a nearby voice. Joe turned to see the person the Rajah had knocked down. He laughed when he saw the chubby face.

"I looked all over for the Rajah, just like Frank told me," Chet Morton said. "But I couldn't find any sign of him. Biff told me you went to the Strand place." He stopped, puzzled, and studied Joe's silk-garbed captive.

"Did I miss something?" Chet asked.

"I can't thank you enough for all your help," Emmett Strand said. He stood with the Hardy boys and Holly in Kennedy International Airport in New York.

"Our pleasure, sir," Frank said. He faced Holly and smiled. "You look good." He hadn't seen her in the six weeks since the Rajah's capture.

She blushed. "Thank you. I'm feeling a lot better these days. I've been getting professional help."

"We both have," Emmett Strand said. "Together. We're close now for the first time in our lives." He held up two airline tickets. "That's why we're taking this trip to Europe. It's about time I stopped worrying about making money and started being friends with my daughter."

He gave Holly a hug. "It's funny. If Paul hadn't tried to destroy me, I would never have known how miserable Holly was. In a way, we're a lot better off."

"So is the Rajah," Joe said. "He'll get lots of help where he is. Maybe they'll even straighten him out someday." But probably not, he thought. At least he's behind bars where he can't do any more harm.

Strand nodded sadly. "It's too bad about him. When I married his mother, I wanted to be a good husband. But it was a mistake. She never really wanted to be married, and when she divorced me, I thought I'd never love anyone again. Until I met Holly's mother.

"The hate that twisted him all those years wasn't necessary. If I had known, I would have been there for him. His mother didn't tell me she was pregnant when she left me. I never knew."

Frank patted his shoulder comfortingly. "Now you've got your daughter back. Make the best of it."

"I'm so glad the murder charges against you were dropped, Joe," Holly said.

Joe shrugged. "It was no big deal. All the Rajah's guards knew he killed Leland. When he turned on them, they turned on him. It wasn't a smart move on your half-brother's part. He may have headed the cult, but Leland was the real brains behind it."

Flight information blared over the airport loudspeakers. "That's our flight, honey," Emmett Strand said. "We've got to go."

"Could I catch up in a minute, Dad?" Holly asked. "I'd like to speak to Frank alone." Her father smiled and nodded, and strolled toward the boarding gates. Smirking, Joe also walked away.

"I just want to thank you again," Holly said when they were alone. "If you hadn't rescued me, I don't know what would have happened. You saved my life, Frank."

"You would have seen the light eventually," he replied.

"I don't think so," she replied. "I only escaped because, for a moment, I thought you loved me. I guess you do, in a way."

It was Frank's turn to blush. "Don't push so hard at love, Holly. You'll find it."

"I already have," she said. "Goodbye, Frank."

She kissed him.

Then she was gone, vanished with her father beyond the boarding gates. Gently he brushed the touch of her off his lips and went to find his brother.

Joe stood at a newsstand, reading a magazine. "It says here that most of the Rajah's followers went back to their families. At least from now on, they'll know better than to think a guru is anything more than just another human being."

"Amen to that," Frank said. They started for the exit.

At the door, a boy approached them. He was dressed in a plain blue suit. He was sixteen at most, and his flame-red hair had recently been cut short, though it had already started to grow again. His hair and the many freckles on his face marked him as Irish-American. In his arm was a stack of books. He didn't recognize Frank or Joe at all.

"Kadji?" Frank said, startled. "Is that you?"

For a moment the boy appeared puzzled. Then he beamed at Frank, though it was obvious he still didn't recognize him. "That was in a past life. I'm called Brother Raphael now."

He thrust a book at them. It was beautifully printed, with a painting of angels battling devils on the cover. "This book reveals the secret struggle that has shaped the history of mankind. I want you to have it. It will show you the role that you are destined to play."

He tried to put the book in Frank's hand. "Our ministry is costly, brother. If you could make a small contribution . . ."

Frank shook his head. "I'm sorry," he said. He pulled his hands back to avoid the book. "I'm sorry for you."

But the boy had already lost interest and, with the book ready, walked toward a young, dark-haired girl wearing blue jeans and carrying a knapsack.

Wordlessly, the Hardys left the airport and went home.

# Be sure to read
## all the books in the
## Hardy Boys Casefiles Series: